A HITMAN IN THE BORGIA BAR

The ocean was high, the moon was full. The *Beatrice Cenci* danced blithely over the waves. The flags fluttering atop, the Gift Galleries gleaming amidship, the frivolities of the staterooms, the gallantries of the crew, all combined to obliterate the realization that there was a well-planned, beautifully designed, solid working ship underneath.

No one dressed for dinner the first night out. Afterwards, Butler sought the bar and remained in it. After this he would be on duty, so to speak, and such indulgences would not be for him.

There were no women in the Borgia Bar tonight. He liked that. Not that he disapproved of women generally, or even of women in bars. It was just that it was too much like work having them around.

Funny how many of his contracts had been women.

Not so odd, though, when you came to think of it. The sort of man who wanted his dirty work done for him tended to have qualms about killing in the first place. Which was why he ordered it done at one or two removes and preferred that it look like an accident.

They never refused to pay the second half of the fee, though. Accidents could happen to anyone.

Bantam offers the finest in classic and modern British murder mysteries.
Ask your bookseller for the books you have missed.

Agatha Christie
Death on the Nile
A Holiday for Murder
The Mousetrap and Other Plays
The Mysterious Affair at Styles
Poirot Investigates
Postern of Fate
The Secret Adversary
The Seven Dials Mystery
Sleeping Murder

Dorothy Simpson
Last Seen Alive
The Night She Died
Puppet for a Corpse
Six Feet Under
Close Her Eyes
coming soon: Element of Doubt

Sheila Radley
The Chief Inspector's Daughter
Death in the Morning
Fate Worse Than Death
Who Saw Him Die?

Elizabeth George
A Great Deliverance
coming soon: A Payment in Blood

Colin Dexter
Last Bus to Woodstock
The Riddle of the Third Mile
The Silent World of Nicholas Quinn
Service of All the Dead
The Dead of Jericho
The Secret of Annexe 3
Last Seen Wearing

John Greenwood
The Mind of Mr. Mosley
The Missing Mr. Mosley
Mosley by Moonlight
Murder, Mr. Mosley
Mists Over Mosley
What, Me, Mr. Mosley?

Ruth Rendell
A Dark-Adapted Eye
    (writing as Barbara Vine)
A Fatal Inversion
    (writing as Barbara Vine)

Marian Babson
Death in Fashion
Reel Murder
Murder, Murder Little Star
Murder on a Mystery Tour
Murder Sails at Midnight

Christianna Brand
Suddenly at His Residence
Heads You Lose

Dorothy Cannell
The Widows Club
coming soon: Down the Garden
    Path

Michael Dibdin
Ratking

MURDER SAILS
AT
MIDNIGHT

Marian Babson

BANTAM BOOKS
NEW YORK • TORONTO • LONDON • SYDNEY • AUCKLAND

This edition contains the complete text
of the original hardcover edition.
NOT ONE WORD HAS BEEN OMITTED.

MURDER SAILS AT MIDNIGHT
A Bantam Book / published by arrangement with the author.

PRINTING HISTORY
William Collins edition published 1975
Bantam edition / May 1989

ISBN 0-553-28096-1

Published simultaneously in the United States and Canada

Bantam Books are published by Bantam Books, a division of Bantam
Doubleday Dell Publishing Group, Inc. Its trademark, consisting of
the words "Bantam Books" and the portrayal of a rooster, is Regis-
tered in U.S. Patent and Trademark Office and in other countries.
Marca Registrada. Bantam Books, 666 Fifth Avenue, New York, New
York 10103.

PRINTED IN THE UNITED STATES OF AMERICA

KR   0 9 8 7 6 5 4 3 2 1

MURDER SAILS
AT
MIDNIGHT

Chapter 1

The man looked around the lunchroom carefully, then slid the large bulky envelope across the table. "There you are," he said. "Half now and the other half when you've done the job. You'll find everything else you need in there, too. The photograph isn't too good—she's camera shy—but you can recognize her from it."

Smiling wryly, Butler slipped the envelope into his briefcase. He didn't bother to count the money, he knew there'd be $2,500 in the envelope. There always was—before the job was done. And it made an attractive gesture, implying trust and good faith, not to count it. The second half—the final payoff—was the one you had to count.

The man looked a bit disconcerted when Butler didn't immediately leave. But the cup of coffee was barely tasted. It had been bought and paid for—why waste it?

"You don't—" the man studied him curiously—"look the sort who'd do this kind of thing for a living."

That was why he came expensive. He could mingle with the victims in their natural habitat—a cocktail party, reception, private view—and not look out of place. Any cheap hood was available for a few hundred to aim a gun or a car at someone—but that could lead to unpleasant questions and suspicions. Too many wealthy hit-and-run victims and even the cops could begin putting two and two together, and take a longer, colder look at the next-of-kin. No, if they wanted a job done with finesse, looking like a bona fide accident, they had to hire a real expert. He cost more, but he was worth it. They were buying long-term insurance—safety for themselves.

"You don't look the sort who'd hire me." Butler returned the compliment, as was expected of him. It paid to keep the clients happy, but it was a lie. You could tell them a mile off. They all had the same greedy discontented twitch around the eyes, the mouth that stretched too quickly into the professionally affable smile of someone accustomed to trying to ingratiate himself with a rich relative. You could walk into a room full of strangers and, after looking around, you could say to yourself: *That one over there. That one is waiting for someone to die.*

"You're sure everything will be all right?"

"Everything will go like clockwork." They didn't want details—people too squeamish to do their own dirty work never did—they just wanted reassurance.

"I hope so, Mr. . . . ?"

"Butler," Butler supplied obligingly. It wasn't the name he had been born with, nor the name he would use aboard ship. It was the name he always used at meetings like this. Clients didn't want him to know their names, but they seemed to feel that it gave them some kind of control over him—a hold, perhaps, an extra insurance against the future—if they knew his. Any name that wasn't Smith or Jones would satisfy them.

It amused him to use Butler. If one of them blundered his end of it after the job was done and the cops caught up with him, what could he tell them? *The Butler did it.*

"I'll be waiting at the other end," the man said. "To pay you the rest of your money and to—and to take care of everything."

Funny, the way they never wanted to say, *Claim the body.* As though they were hiding what they were doing, even from themselves. As though it were just another business transaction. That was probably why so much of the jargon of business had crept into it.

"Fine." Butler finished his coffee, dabbed meticulously at his mouth with the paper napkin, and stood up.

"Mister . . ." Butler held out his hand, waiting. Sometimes it was a long wait, but it was something he personally always insisted on. It sealed the bargain, made them irrevocably part of it, brought home to them what they were doing.

It wasn't as long as some of the waits he had had. Eventually, they always held out their hand—if they didn't want to back out of it. The other man shrugged and slowly put out his hand now.

"Mister . . ." Butler took it in a firm grip. "You've got yourself a contract."

Chapter 2

The *Beatrice Cenci* sailed at midnight.

Which was not nearly so romantic as it sounded, Valerie Meadows thought, trying to manoeuvre the wheelchair through the crowds of people and piles of luggage.

The people made way, once they noticed she was trying to get through, glancing at her incuriously; then, with more curiosity, at the wheelchair. Once again, she appreciated the anonymity given by a nurse's uniform. No one looked at her face, just at the crisp white cap and the flicker of white showing beneath the navy cloak. Registering "nurse," they turned their eyes with concealed avidity to the more interesting and dramatic point—the occupant of the wheelchair, the patient.

Mrs. Abercrombie was sitting bolt upright, head high, ignoring the curious stares with regal disdain. But she was tiring. The small, almost involuntary brushing-aside motions of her hands betrayed that. At home, that would be the signal for her step-niece and nephew to say goodnight, drop a kiss on her cheek, and withdraw. In the crowded departure hall, taken out of context, her gestures simply looked ineffectual and fretful.

An occasional stranger, bolder than the others, would glance from the wheelchair to the steeply-pitched gangplank which the early arrivals were already crossing from shore to ship, and try to meet Valerie's eyes with a look which was intended to convey sympathy—or even an offer of help.

Valerie avoided their eyes—she'd had a lot of practice at that exercise over the past few months. And their sympathy was unnecessary.

4

The chauffeur had gone ahead to make the necessary arrangements. Once she and Mrs. Abercrombie had cleared the Reservation Desk and Immigration, he would rejoin them. Together, they would take Mrs. Abercrombie and wheelchair across the almost-level gangplank the longshoremen were using to load luggage into the bows of the ship. Then they would go up in the freight elevator with the cabin luggage to the upper deck where Mrs. Abercrombie's suite was waiting. These things were all more swiftly and easily arranged than casual travellers ever realized.

Mrs. Abercrombie's head had begun to turn restlessly from side to side. She hated having what she considered her weakness on display—and she *was* growing stronger. The decision to keep her confined to a wheelchair for a while longer had been the doctor's, not hers. Although even she had had to agree that it would spare her much strain and effort during the always-tedious embarkation period. When she returned home, after her winter on the Riviera, she had promised her family that she would walk off the ship—and she undoubtedly would. It would take more than a heart attack to defeat Mrs. Abercrombie.

Mrs. Abercrombie raised her hand again and this time the gesture was imperative. Valerie stopped pushing, put on the brake and went round to the front of the chair to collect Mrs. Abercrombie's passport and ticket. They were very close to the Reservation Desk now.

"So much noise," Mrs. Abercrombie complained. "So many people."

"We'll be on board soon," Valerie comforted. She agreed with Mrs. Abercrombie—there were too many people. Or, perhaps what Mrs. Abercrombie meant was: none of them were the right people. It would be different if some of the people in this crowd had come to see *her* off.

But Mrs. Abercrombie had said her good-byes at a family dinner last night. She had spent today resting.

Val had spent it writing letters. There were no good-byes for her—there never had been, not even a few months ago when she left the small mid-Western city where she had once thought she might spend the rest of her life. Now

5

she was on her way back to England—the long way round. New York to Genoa, Genoa to Mentone, Mentone—after Mrs. Abercrombie had settled and had found a new nurse—to Paris. Then Paris to London—home.

There would be smiling faces to greet her—to blot out the memory of the faces distorted with anger and hatred that had watched her from behind fluffy net curtains as she walked down the twisting path from the big house on the hill for the last time. There would be voices speaking her name with welcome, with laughter—to blur the remembered sound of other voices, cold tight voices insinuating unimaginable accusations . . .

"Yes, Mrs. Abercrombie, I'm sorry—" Val came back to the present, to the crush of strangers, the multi-lingual babble of voices, the embraces all around them, the laughter, the tears.

". . . out of here," Mrs. Abercrombie repeated. "Where's Edwards?"

"He's coming now." The chauffeur was shouldering his way through the crowd. He carried a sheaf of long-stemmed red roses.

"From Mr. Augustus and Miss Mildred, ma'am." He placed the sheaf on Mrs. Abercrombie's lap reverentially.

"Oh, bother?" Mrs. Abercrombie looked down at the roses without appreciation. "I *told* them no flowers." She sounded as annoyed as though any previous conduct of her step-niece and nephew had ever given her any indication that they were obedient to her wishes.

"Never mind," Val soothed. "We'll soon be aboard and put them in water. They'll be quite nice to have in the cabin on the way across—cheerful." She looked a question at Edwards and he nodded.

"They'll be ready for us as soon as we've finished here." She released the brake and began edging the wheelchair forward again.

"So many people," Mrs. Abercrombie fretted again. "So many children."

"They won't all be aboard," Val said. "Most of them will just be here seeing relatives off."

6

She hoped she spoke the truth. Some groups surrounding elderly people were obviously having a memorable outing, saying what would probably be their last farewells to grandparents—perhaps great-grandparents—returning to the Old Country. Excited youngsters, allowed to stay up to this unprecedented hour, were milling about, playing tag, shouting for attention, whining for treats, bursting into tears. They were alternately cuffed and embraced by harassed parents having difficulties with their own emotions.

Inevitably, some of these children would be here because they were sailing. However, few of these, if any, would be travelling First Class. In fact, First Class was rapidly becoming an anachronism in today's world, where the least sophisticated realized that passengers in Tourist Class arrived at the same time as First Class passengers; and people who had the money for First Class now felt it pretentious and a vague insult to the Third World to spend that money in such a manner. The *Beatrice Cenci*, like most of the recent liners, was designed and outfitted to conform to the new order. She was almost completely a one-class ship—Tourist Class. There were accommodations for possibly as many as twenty-five diehards who insisted on travelling in the greatest luxury that could be afforded, but First Class was rarely fully booked. It would not be for this voyage.. There had been an almost embarrassing choice of accommodation available, despite the last-minute impulsiveness of Mrs. Abercrombie's decision.

It came to Val with a feeling of vague surprise that she could have afforded to travel First Class on her own, had she been so minded. As a passenger, paying the full fare and with no duties attached. It was one of those thoughts that now and then swept over her, bringing with it a realization that wealth was hers now and she might even be able to enjoy it some day—if only the manner of acquiring could recede into distant memory and eventually be forgotten.

But not right now. She had committed herself to working her passage taking care of Mrs. Abercrombie. Something deep within her wondered if she had taken on this

7

task as a sort of penance. Something else told her that she wanted—was happier with—a patient to look after right now. She needed Mrs. Abercrombie, perhaps more than Mrs. Abercrombie needed her.

"Watch where you're going, girl!" Mrs. Abercrombie's cry came in time to save her from being wheeled into a small cluster of Italian-Americans surrounding a couple with their baby.

"Sorry," Val apologized.

"That's all right." The woman with the baby smiled at her, radiating excitement. "Aren't midnight sailings thrilling? And Guido is being so *good*—" She turned away to nuzzle the complacent baby in her arms. "He's going to turn out to be a born traveller—I just know it."

"Honestly, Gloria," her sister said. "You're going to spoil that kid."

"Why not?" Gloria laughed. "I waited long enough for him." Her eyes turned to meet a pair of darker eyes hovering above her head. "For both of you."

There was a burst of laughter from the group. "Honestly, Gloria," her sister said. "You sound like a teenager." With ten years of marriage behind her, and five kids to her credit, she could afford to be condescendingly amused. It wasn't an unhoped-for miracle for her.

"Now, remember," her mother said. "The package in the gold foil is for Grandma Emilia, the black-and-silver stripes goes to Cousin Luigi, the red tissue belongs to Aunt Anna, the dark brown—Gloria, you're not listening."

"Yes, I am, Ma. But you've told me all this before."

"Never mind, it's important. Here—" Her mother dived into her handbag and surfaced with a folded piece of paper. "I've made a list so you don't forget. Put it away somewhere where you can't lose it. Tags can fall off, you know, and we don't want to get those presents mixed up."

"All right, Ma." Gloria tucked the paper into her own handbag, with a little moue at her husband. Later, they would have a few minutes alone in her cabin before the "All ashore" sounded. She felt a pang at the thought. Once, she had been used to travelling alone, but after having had a man around for the past two years, it would never be the same again. *But I'm not really alone,* the unexpected thought cheered her. *I've got Guido.*

"You will be all right, all by yourself?" As though he had been following her thoughts, Lorenzo frowned down at her anxiously.

"I'm not a baby," she laughed. "I *have* travelled before."

As soon as the words were spoken, she knew it was the wrong thing to have said. The familiar black thundercloud moved across his face—he hated to be reminded of the time when she had not known him, had had no idea of his existence. Any careless reference to those days brought on the black, brooding mood that it could sometimes take her the rest of the evening to dispel.

But they didn't have the rest of the evening now. She would be going aboard at any minute, sailing, leaving him behind. Nor did they have the necessary privacy.

"She got along just fine before." Her brother-in-law seemed determined to worsen the situation, underlining the obvious. "One of the best little businesswomen in New York. Never came back from a buying trip without showing at least two hundred per cent profit. Just like old times, eh, kid?" His elbow sank into Gloria's ribs. "Oh, those buying trips!"

Gloria bared her teeth at him and moved out of range of that thrusting elbow. Her personal opinion that he was a bore, a slob, and devoid of any sense of humour had often been agreed with by Lorenzo. Unfortunately, that did not prevent Lorenzo from taking him seriously—and always at the wrong moment.

A tall, rather handsome man in ship's uniform moved past on his way to the gangplank. He smiled at the baby, at Gloria, at everyone—and seemed about to speak.

Lorenzo glared at him ferociously, challenging him to dare to make an overture towards *his* child, *his* wife. The officer moved his shoulders indifferently. He had seen jealous husbands before, his shrug said. He gave Gloria a merry wink. And, when they were *that* jealous, the wink said,

9

they were on to a good thing—and maybe leaving the Good Thing to travel alone.

Gloria looked away quickly, but Lorenzo had already caught the wink. He wasn't the only one.

"How about that?" her brother-in-law shouted. "Not even aboard yet—and she's started already!" His heavy-handed pretence that, once away from home, she behaved as he would have liked to had always been tedious and irritating. With Lorenzo in his present mood, it was disastrous.

"You have met him before? On another ship, another voyage?" Lorenzo glowered hatred after the officer. When he looked down at her again, the hatred was still in his gaze. It was one of the times when it seemed as though he hated her.

"Don't be silly," Gloria said quickly. "I've never seen him before in my life."

"He will be aboard." Mordantly, Lorenzo watched the dapper figure now crossing the gangplank to the ship unhurriedly.

"That's right, boy! Don't let her—"

"Joe—" Pauline tugged at her husband's arm, evidently beginning to realize that he had gone too far, that Lorenzo had stopped seeing the joke.

"You've got to watch her every minute—ooof!" He gave Pauline an injured look, rubbing his side.

"Why don't we all go on board now?" Her mother had also noticed the warning signs that this was more likely to wind up as a family fight than a fond farewell.

"Great!" There was no doubt about it, Joe had overdone the farewell toasts by at least three to one of everybody else's. "I want to give that officer a friendly warning. He doesn't know who he's mixing with, does he, boy?"

It was another of Joe's tiresome pretences that Lorenzo, because he came from Sicily, had a direct linkup with the Mafia and could have anyone who became troublesome "taken care of." It was too bad it wasn't true—a light working-over might do Joe a world of good.

"We'll see you on board," Gloria said firmly. "You know the cabin number, don't you, Ma? You go ahead and sit down. I've still got some formalities here—no sense in all of us standing around."

"I will stay with you." Lorenzo took little Guido from her arms and glared around at the crowd, as though every single male in it was a prospective threat to his family honour.

"I was hoping you would," Gloria reassured him instantly. Thankfully, she watched Pauline call the older kids back from the magazine stand where they had been choosing comic books and begin herding them towards the gangplank. "We aren't going to have much time alone together, I can see."

"You will write every day!" Lorenzo commanded. "You will write and tell me how my son is. You will write the first letter tomorrow."

"All right," Gloria laughed. "But you do realize, don't you, that I won't be able to mail the letters until the ship lands? They don't have any mail boxes in mid-Atlantic."

"It does not matter." Lorenzo's jaw set in a stubborn line. "You will write every day!"

"Okay, okay—if it makes you happy." Absently, Gloria searched through her handbag and pulled out a lipstick. She halted when she saw his suspicious look.

"Who do you make yourself beautiful for?"

"I was only getting out my ticket." Guiltily, she let the lipstick slide back. Millions of nice, tractable, biddable American men around and she had to wind up with an old-fashioned Italian rule-the-roost jealous husband. Still, she had to admit, she'd had her chances at a few of those Americans and found them so tame and pallid that she'd decided she'd be happier single—until she met Lorenzo.

Perhaps in a few more years, when he grew more sure of her—and of himself—his possessiveness would lessen.

"You have not lost it?"

"It's right here." Her fingers curled around it a little too tightly, creasing it. It was another bone of contention— all that money—just to travel First Class. It would cut down on the profits on *this* buying trip, and she'd have some fun trying to justify it on her Income Tax Return—she'd

11

never bothered to travel First Class before and her Tax Office knew it, they had it on her past returns. It was simply pandering to Lorenzo's stupid male pride again—he'd insisted that she go First Class. And it wasn't as though he were paying for it.

"Good." Lorenzo smiled with as much satisfaction as though he *had* footed the bill.

"There's nothing good about it." Sheer irritation at his attitude made her snap. "It's too damned expensive. It was unnecessary, and I won't enjoy a minute of it."

"Enjoy?" That had wiped the smile off his face. "You are leaving me to *enjoy*?"

"You know what I mean." She hadn't intended to quarrel about it again, but everything was getting out of hand. That lout, Joe, had started it and now it had taken on an impetus of its own.

"No!" He turned away, as though he would stride from the dock, taking the baby with him. It was one of the unadmitted terrors of her life: that, some day, in one of his tempers, he would leave, taking Guido back to Italy with him, and then there would be a desperate struggle through Italian Courts where the ingrained attitude was that the son belonged to his father, that the mother counted as nothing, no matter how much of a better life should could offer . . .

"Lorenzo." She pulled herself together, *she* was the one going to Italy with little Guido, and it would be a couple of months before Lorenzo saw them again. No wonder he was upset.

"Lorenzo—" She touched his arm, turning him back to her. "This is no time to quarrel."

"No." He looked down at her, frowning in the struggle to find enough English to convey what he wanted to say. "I know. Some day, *I* pay. Some day, I make enough money, *I* pay all bills. But now—"

"It's all right, Lorenzo. I understand."

"It is right—" Lorenzo still struggled determinedly with the language he was determined to conquer— "that my son goes First Class. He must always go First Class. My son is special."

"I agree. He's my son, too, remember." She smiled up at him, trying to coax him back to a pleasant mood before they joined the others. "And what about me?"

"Yes." He studied her with a curiously blank glare for a moment, refusing to be placated. Something sparked deep at the back of his eyes. "You are special, too."

She recoiled instinctively, for no reason she could put a name to, and felt—with horror—her heel crunch down on someone's foot.

"Oh, I'm so *sorry!*" Gloria whirled about, her hand stretched out to steady her unfortunate, and unintended victim.

"It's all right." The other girl's face was pale.

"But I *hurt* you. Are you—?"

"It's all right," the girl repeated. She had a cool, crisp English voice. "It wasn't your fault. It's always the same in a crowd like this—pushing and milling about . . ." She began to move away.

"I *did* hurt you," Gloria cried in consternation. "You're limping!"

"That's not your fault," Susan Emery said. "I've always limped."

She should not have said it—that poor woman looked absolutely stricken with embarrassment at her clumsiness. Apart from which, it wasn't strictly true. She had spent the first fourteen years of her life with two legs as good and straight as anyone else's. Two feet that hit the ground at the same angle, giving her a smooth, attractive gait she had never appreciated—until it was gone forever.

"Susan—over here!" They were waiting at the foot of the gangplank, those American friends from whom she had been momentarily separated by her mishap.

"Look—" Betty gestured towards the forward gangplank where the longshoremen were loading luggage. "That woman in the wheelchair *is* going on board. She must be making the voyage—I can't imagine her bothering, otherwise—and there's a nurse in attendance. You might have some drama on board before you land."

"I'd rather not," Susan said. "Life has been dramatic

enough lately. I long for peace and quiet on the crossing."
But her eyes automatically followed the figures on the lower
gangplank, assessing them. This was the time when people
began to sort themselves out, and idle speculations on
which were to be fellow passengers and which were merely
seeing off friends were proved false or confirmed. It had
always been fairly certain that the woman in the wheelchair
was to be a passenger—she had been too aloof from the
crowd, with only uniformed servants beside her. Undoubtedly, the woman would also be a First Class passenger. It
was unlikely, however, that she would take her meals in the
dining salon, or be much in evidence. Any dramas revolving around her would take place in the privacy of her own
stateroom. For which relief, much thanks.

"Careful—" They began shepherding her up the gangplank with exaggerated care. "Don't fall off the ship." They
shrieked with laughter.

They had thought the staid, archaic phrasing of the
Will hilarious. American Wills were solemn enough, but
the English variety, with its painstaking provision for every
eventuality, had seemed to them so funny as to be unreal.

"Listen—" Betty, one of her flatmates, had read out
portions of it. "Just *listen* to this: 'PROVIDED ALWAYS that my
said daughter SUSAN MARGOT EMERY shall survive me for
the space of three months. If not, she shall be deemed to
have predeceased me. IN WHICH CASE—' How about that?"

"It's because of death duties," Susan had tried to explain. "So that the estate won't be landed with two lots of
death duties in case an accident should happen to me."

"Are you sure?" Their laughter rose and fell. "It sounds
as though he expects someone to try to bump you off."

"Nothing of the sort." (Eric's face rose mockingly at the
back of her mind.) "It's a standard procedure solicitors have
used ever since death duties were first introduced. It's very
sensible."

". . . 'IN WHICH CASE—,'" Betty continued relentlessly. "'I GIVE DEVISE AND BEQUEATH unto my nephew
ERIC MAXIMILIAN HOLMES-EMERY all my property both
real and personal whatsoever and wheresoever of which I

die possessed—' That sounds like the best motive I ever heard for getting rid of someone. How do you get along with this cousin, anyway? I never heard you mention him."

"We're on speaking terms." The chill in her voice warned them that the joke was growing dangerously thin. Despite the period of estrangement, it was, after all, her father who had just died.

"Sorry." Betty handed back the legal parchment, its red seals gleaming like drops of fresh blood beside the signatures of the witnesses. "It just seems so odd to our American eyes."

"It's all right." She met the apology half-way. "It's just that—"

"You're upset, of course." Betty looked at her anxiously. "What are you going to do? I mean, do you want to fly home tomorrow or—?"

"No, there's no point to that." They had already held the funeral—before Eric had seen fit to write to her. It had seemed best that way, he had said. There were no decisions for her to take, everything had been prearranged with the solicitors. There would, of course, be formalities connected with the estate, but there was no great urgency about them, the Will had to go through Probate first. She could return at her leisure.

"I might as well take my holiday first." She saw Betty sag with relief. Four of them from the office had hired a cottage in the Adirondacks for two weeks, it would not have been easy to find a replacement if she had dropped out of the arrangement at this late date. "Then I can give my notice when I get back and work out the month before I leave."

Unacknowledged at the back of her mind, something ticked off the timing she was indicating. He had been dead for two weeks before the letter reached her; it would be another week before their holiday. Two weeks of holiday, then a month working out her notice upon their return. (It was not strictly necessary to give a month's notice in New York, but no one in England would realize that.) That would give her a week at home to pack and make final preparations before the sailing she had booked—the only one available now that the big liners didn't work the Atlantic run during the winter months, but found it more financially rewarding to go cruising instead. Nearly a week on board the *Beatrice Cenci*—a five-day crossing, bringing her into Genoa. She would spend a few days in Italy, a few more in Paris. So that, by the time she reached England, she would have already safely survived the three-month period. The estate would be hers when she met Eric again. Hers, to dipose of as she liked in a Will of her own—and Eric would never be her heir and he knew it. Once she had survived that three-month period, she was safe . . .

"Don't stand there in a trance!" Betty poked her in the back. "There's a freezing wind coming up the Hudson here. Not to mention the people behind us who want to go on board."

"Sorry." She took a firm grip on the handrail and began to climb the gangplank, being careful to avoid the raised slats which bisected the boards horizontally at intervals of eighteen inches or so. They were meant to prevent slipping in wet weather, or help the passengers when the incline was particularly steep. They didn't help her; slowed her, rather.

Behind her, she heard a murmur as her limp was noticed and remarked on by the passengers waiting to board. She had grown accustomed to this reaction, but never resigned to it. Not that it mattered—few of them would be travelling First Class. Ordinarily, she wouldn't have herself, but Eric had insisted, saying the estate could well afford it and that she owed herself a bit of luxury after being a hard-working girl in New York for the past three years. Perhaps he was right.

Holding her head a little higher and struggling to control the protesting leg, which was already aching from all the standing around and the unaccustomed pitch of the steep gangplank, she moved a little faster.

Her steps seemed to keep pace with the sonorous phrases drumming through her mind: "PROVIDED ALWAYS that my said daughter SUSAN MARGOT EMERY . . ."

Chapter 3

Butler had been one of the first on board. He liked it that way. It gave him time for an unhurried preliminary exploration of the layout. In the increasing flood of people pouring aboard, seeking cabin numbers, hunting farewell parties, he would not be noticed or remembered. That was the advantage of a nondescript face with no identifying marks.

Later, when the passengers themselves were settling down, he would move more cautiously to ascertain that the correct passenger was assigned to the cabin according to his information. Later still, when the passenger list was distributed on the second or third day out, he would make a final cross-check. He was meticulous on points like these. You didn't collect on the wrong body. And, on board ship, too many people didn't wind up in the same cabin they started out in. They imagined they were too near the engines, or the cooking smells, or that the ship would seem steadier from another location, and so they went running to the purser who, if at all possible, would find them alternative accommodation—purely for the sake of shutting them up, if for no other reason.

It was better not to make a move until everyone had settled down and been lulled into somnambulance by the quiet monotony of shipboard routine. It was better, in any case, not to make a move until they were well out to sea.

Meanwhile, the preliminary reconnaissance over, Butler stood in a shadowed hollow by a smokestack on the uppermost deck and looked down on the floodlit pier, watching the passengers come aboard.

It was a game he had enjoyed even when a child: the

stalker, observing without being observed. Now it was part of his living, and he enjoyed it still.

He lit a cigarette, cupping both hands around the match, not so much to shield the flame from the wind as to hide his face which might be seen too clearly in the brief flare of light. He pitched the spent match over the side, imagining the tiny "plop" the match would make as it slipped into the Hudson far below.

The newspaper photograph had been blurred, but he thought he would recognize her when he saw her. Not that it was important to spot her in advance—they would be cast away together on this floating island for nearly a week, and she would not be able to escape—but it was a matter of pride to him that he do so.

She might have come on board already, while he was strolling down strange companionways, finding the pool, the library, the dining salon, the cabin. But he didn't think so. Already he was placing his mental bets on the likely behaviour of his quarry, trying to get inside her mind, see things as she would see them, think the way she thought, ascertain her strengths and weaknesses, if any. There would be plenty of time to study her, of course, but he liked the excitement of those private initial bets, the feeling of satisfaction when he was proved right. This one, now, he was betting would not be one of the early birds—she was in no particular hurry. His chips were on that number, and the little wheel was beginning to spin.

Below decks, the engines coughed and throbbed, switching into a more businesslike, purposeful rhythm. The ship stirred and seemed to give a little skip, as though an unexpectedly high wave had swelled beneath it. The crew began moving among the crowds with brisker steps.

Butler moved forward to the rail. Time was getting close. He looked down, both gangplanks were in view, a steady stream coming aboard. Overhead, cables creaked as cranes swung their loads of heavy crates up, over, and down into the cargo hold. Momentarily, he was diverted as he watched the longshoremen drive a neat little orange Fiat on to the loading platform and begin to secure the cables

18

around it. Coals to Newcastle, you'd think. Unless the owner were an emigrant, returning in triumph with prizes he could not have won in his native village. More likely, though, it was a second or third generation American, not quite realizing that his car would be less of a status symbol in its own country.

Then he saw her. All other thoughts dissolved like the chimera they were. This was real. All his concentration burned down on that slight figure below. As though sensing something strange, she seemed to hesitate in her progress and raised her head.

Quickly, he stepped back into the shadows. He had seen enough. He frowned. More than enough—he hadn't been told about that. Just a little item the customer had forgotten to mention—or been ashamed to.

Butler lit another cigarette from the stub of the old one before pitching it over the side, watching the red arc of its descent, scattering fiery ashes as though to jettison its live tip before hitting the oily surface of the Hudson. This would take some thinking about.

It changed things. Not the basic fact—she was still his contract, and he prided himself on executing his contracts. But it made things different. Whether easier or harder remained to be seen. For one thing, it opened up a whole new era of weakness—a vulnerability which might be used against her when the time came.

Abruptly the public address system crackled into life with the first of the "All ashore" warnings. "Will all visitors kindly leave the ship . . . Will all visitors . . ." It was repeated in Italian. There was a high-pitched hum of consternation from the decks below him and a few of the more easily panicked began to fight their way down the gangplank against the still oncoming stream. The more experienced lingered, knowing that the announcement would be repeated at least twice more, at ten- or fifteen-minute intervals. There was no immediate hurry. For one thing, they were still loading cargo. Butler lit another cigarette . . .

"Will all visitors . . ." A note midway between desperation and exasperation had entered the metallic voice. The cranes had rolled back from the dock's edge, the cover had been replaced on the cargo hatch and bolted down. ". . . *Please* . . . will all visitors . . ."

One of the crew materialized suddenly near Butler, standing by to cast off the hawser looped over a stanchion. Butler froze, motionless. He had not been noticed.

Tugboats were getting up steam below, nuzzling up against the *Beatrice Cenci* fore and aft, ready to edge her away from the dock and out into the deep current of the river. They tooted and the deep commanding whistle of the *Beatrice Cenci* signalled back imperiously.

Passengers began lining the railing now, waving to those on shore. There was a gigantic creaking sigh as the gangplank was winched away from the ship, severing its frail connection with the land.

Suddenly, the *Beatrice Cenci* took on new life, riding high, dancing on tiptoe to break away, move out into her proper element. Again her whistle blasted, celebrating the removal of the last fetters binding her to the shore.

"*Good-bye* . . ." From the pier, they began throwing last kisses, shouting final frantic messages to those aboard. "*Don't forget to write . . .*"

Rippling, oil-slicked water gleamed in a widening triangle as the tugs nosed the prow of the *Beatrice Cenci* out into midstream, beginning to turn her, set her on her course.

"*Don't forget my Venetian glass . . .*"

The sailor slipped the loop off the stanchion, tossing it overboard. There was a sharp slap as it hit the water.

"*Take care . . .*" The cries from shore were fainter now, as though the criers were beginning to realize that they were fading away, blurring into the landscape, already faintly unreal.

Only the *Beatrice Cenci* was real now, throbbing into life, assuming her proper identity, becoming an entity in her own right.

"*Don't*—" One last message from shore rose above all the others in laughing urgency. "*Don't fall off the ship . . .*"

In the darkness, Butler smiled.

Chapter 4

Breakfast was informal. Later in the morning, tables would be assigned to the passengers and they would then keep to their own table for the remainder of the voyage. But, for this morning's breakfast, you could sit anywhere.

Gloria chose an empty table. That way, if anyone objected to Guido, they didn't have to sit with them. She hoped she would draw congenial table companions, but wondered about it a bit nervously. In more recent years, all her trips had been by air. It was good to be back on a ship again, but she couldn't help recalling uneasily that, on her early voyages, there had always been a refugee or two from First Class prowling restlessly around the fringes of Tourist activities, claiming, "They're all a bunch of snobs up there."

It seemed all right at the moment. A beaming steward had rushed up with a high chair for Guido and reassured her earnestly as to the quality and freshness of the orange juice. Of course, that was one of the advantages of travelling on an Italian ship—children were loved and approved of, rather than just tolerated on a nuisance level somewhere below that of dogs, who could be shut up out of the way in the kennels at the rear of the sun deck.

"Pardon?" A hesitant voice broke into her thoughts. "Is it all right to sit here?"

Gloria looked up to see black cloth, a Roman collar, a nondescript diffident face. Someone else who wasn't sure of his welcome. Although, again, more secure and respected on an Italian liner than he might be on another.

"Sit down, Father," she said, a trifle more warmly than was necessary, just to show him that it was really all right. "We don't have any special places this morning. It's all informal."

"Thank you." Smiling his relief, he sank into a chair opposite and picked up the menu.

Once more the beaming steward rushed forward, giving the impression that, with a bambino and a padre both at his table, his cup was overflowing. Radiating approval of all concerned, he took their orders and dashed away.

"It's a beautiful morning," the padre said.

"Beautiful," Gloria agreed, a little natural wariness creeping into her voice. The trouble with becoming friendly with any priests on board ship, she remembered now, was that they then expected to find you at their Mass every morning. Since the natural inclination of both priest and ship's personnel was to get the whole business over and out of everyone's way as quickly as possible, this tended to mean that he was assigned a cinema or smoking-room for 7:00 or 7:30 a.m. An inconvenient enough hour at any time, but an increasingly intolerable one when the clocks were put ahead an hour every night and one was supposed to be on vacation anyway. What was a vacation if you weren't able to sleep late?

Guido gurgled and Gloria turned to him gratefully. She had almost forgotten that things were different now. She had a baby with her and therefore could not reasonably be expected to desert the child at the break of dawn—not even for Mass. Catching her mood, and responding to it, Guido chortled with delight and reached out towards her. She let him capture her hand and drum it against his tray, laughing with him.

"Lovely child," the padre said. "Boy or girl?"

"Boy," Gloria said. "His name is Guido."

"A good name," he smiled. "I'm a James, myself. James—" he hesitated. "James Service."

"And I'm Gloria Pontini—Gloria Grandi Pontini." She wondered momentarily if he had expected her to say something else. He looked both relieved and a little uncomfortable.

The steward brought their orange juice just then and set it before them. Automatically, Gloria picked up Guido's and turned to him, then stopped and half-guiltily turned back to her table companion.

"Sorry, Father," she murmured, but he did not appear to have noticed. He had already drained his own glass—had he momentarily dipped his head before picking it up? Not that it mattered. If he wasn't prepared to be starchy about saying grace, who was she to complain? It helped to make life a bit easier.

Guido gave a peremptory cry, his anxious eyes fixed on the glass in his mother's hand.

"Sorry, darling." She steadied the glass of orange juice at his lips, ignoring hands that tried to strike hers aside and grasp it for himself. That was all very well on shore with plastic mugs, but not here.

Bacon and eggs appeared almost immediately, along with a bowl of oatmeal for Guido.

"No egg for the young man?" Father Service enquired interestedly.

"Not until I find out how good a sailor he is," Gloria said. "This is his first trip. I hope he's got a steady stomach. He's all right in a car, so there's a good chance he has."

"It's all in the mind," Father Service declared firmly. "Half of these people come on board convinced they're going to be seasick, and so they will be."

"Yes." She had heard that theory before. Frequently, those who voiced it were flat on their backs in their bunks before mid-voyage.

"Yes, your Guido's a sensible little chap—and no one can get at him to worry him about being sick. He'll be all right."

"I hope so." She glanced out of the nearest porthole at the sun sparkling on the water. "Anyway, we're off to a fine start. It's nice and calm today."

"It is," he agreed, buttering a piece of toast and looking out at the morning with as much satisfaction as though he had ordered it especially for them. "It's a beautiful day."

"It's a beautiful day, Mrs. Abercrombie." Val drew back the curtains over the porthole. Automatically, she reached

23

to open it, but the forbidding complications of nuts and bolts defeated her. Also, there was a notice requesting passengers to call their cabin steward if they wanted their porthole open and not to attempt it themselves. In the unlikely event that they *could*, Val thought, turning back into the stateroom.

Mrs. Abercrombie had struggled upwards against the pillows to a sitting position and was resting there now as though the effort had depleted her resources. She smiled a faint "Good morning" and closed her eyes again.

"Don't get up," Val said, in some concern—yesterday *had* been a very tiring day. "I'll ring for the cabin steward. We can have breakfast here."

"*You* needn't," Mrs. Abercrombie said. She sat a bit straighter, her voice sounded stronger. "I shall be quite all right. You'll want to eat in the dining salon, look over your fellow passengers, explore the ship. You run along. The cabin steward can look after me well enough for breakfast."

"Well . . ." Valerie was tempted. It was going to be a glorious day—tomorrow it might be raining. The weather was tricky and unpredictable so late in the year.

"Go along," Mrs. Abercrombie said. "You can do some chores if it will make you feel less guilty. I'll want a deckchair reserved in a sheltered corner. And you can get our table—I don't intend to take all my meals in this cabin."

There was a tap and the door swung inward. "Good morning, signora." The cabin steward looked as bright and sparkling as the day outside. "You ring?"

"I'd like some breakfast," Mrs. Abercrombie said.

"Ah, you not seasick?" He advanced farther into the cabin. "Good."

"Toast and coffee," Mrs. Abercrombie ordered. "Perhaps some scrambled eggs."

"Immediately, signora." He sketched a bow and withdrew.

"Well," Mrs. Abercrombie said dubiously, "the service *seems* all right."

"I'm sure it will be," Val assured her. "Would you like the porthole opened when he comes back?"

"Not worth the trouble," Mrs. Abercrombie said. "I shall be going on deck this afternoon." She looked at Val and frowned. "Why do you wear your uniform? It isn't necessary. You ought to wear something more comfortable for shipboard."

"It doesn't matter," Val said.

"Why don't you go and change?" Mrs. Abercrombie insisted. "You'll be happier in a sweater and skirt. Slacks, if you prefer. *I* shan't mind."

"No," Val threw her own words back at her. "Not worth the trouble." She recognized the beginning of one of those silent battles one often had with a patient. Mrs. Abercrombie did not want to be made conspicuous as the shipboard invalid. The wheelchair would not seem quite so confining if pushed by a girl in ordinary clothes, who might be a devoted daughter, niece, secretary or companion. A girl in nurse's uniform, however, immediately pointed her out as under medical care—perhaps dangerously ill. It would make her the centre of nervous eyes, watching to see if she were going to live or die—and she had had enough of that.

"Perhaps later," Val said, not really intending to relent. She needed the protective coloration of a uniform. No one looked twice at a nurse's face. She, too, had had more than her share of watching eyes. But she could not tell Mrs. Abercrombie that.

She gathered up her cloak when the brisk tap at the door signalled the entrance of the cabin steward with Mrs. Abercrombie's tray.

"You'll be all right now. I'll have my breakfast in the dining salon and arrange for our deck-chairs, then I'll come back for you."

"Yes, yes," Mrs. Abercrombie said, her patience fraying. "Run along and don't *fuss* so." She aimed a deceptive smile at the steward pouring her coffee, as she added with very little truth, "I'm perfectly all right."

Val closed the door quietly behind her and stepped out into the passage. The faint roll of the ship was more discernible out here, the floor seeming to rise to meet her feet as a cat arches her neck into a caress. Already, she felt her walk begin to change, to assume the looseness that allowed her to roll with the motion and not feel off-balance.

At the far end of the corridor, she was conscious of one of the uniformed officers standing watching her progress. She pulled her face into the blank protective mask she had learned to hide behind so well in the recent past and looked beyond him as she approached.

She had expected him to move out of her way. Instead, he stepped forward.

"Miss Meadows?"

"Yes." She did not look directly at him, but was aware of his gaze. He frowned, as though displeased at her indifference. Or, perhaps, trying to reconcile her face with the blurred photographs which had appeared in so many news- papers.

"A message for you, Miss Meadows." She saw now that he held out a cablegram to her. "It came over the wireless a few minutes ago."

"Thank you." She took it, expressionless, further disappointing him by not glancing at it. She slipped it unopened into her pocket.

Had Ralphie traced her here? If the message was a resumption of hostilities, repeating some of the vituperation he had showered on her during those last few days—

She pulled her mind back from a perilous edge. No one had seen her break down—and no one would. Did the officer know the contents of her cable and was that the reason for part of his disappointment? Had he expected a fine dramatic scene when she read the cable?

She smiled vaguely at him and moved away. He stepped back to let her pass, gesturing her forward with a flourish of his arm. The cuff of his jacket was stiff with gold braid. It caught her attention; whatever rank could he hold? This brought in its train a further disquiet: surely officers of that rank didn't act as messenger boys? There must be stewards or cabin boys to deliver messages.

Even now, she was aware of his eyes boring into her back. Perhaps he *had* expected a scene. All the more reason for not opening her cablegram until she was once more within the privacy of her stateroom.

Meanwhile, she found the stairs leading to the dining salon and began to descend them. There was enough to occupy her. Bad news could always wait.

Susan Emery heard the ship stirring around her. The soft chime of bells to announce breakfast had rung a short time ago and now footsteps were passing along the corridor outside. She would have tea and toast in her cabin, she decided, but not quite yet.

For the moment it was enough to lie back and enjoy the feeling of release being aboard ship gave one. Whatever was happening elsewhere in the world, one was absolved from the responsibility of having to do anything about it. Moreover, there was literally nothing one *could* do. For the next five days the world had shrunk down to the floating island of the *Beatrice Cenci*. A warm, womblike world where all one's comforts were attended to, where nothing more unpleasant than being caught for half an hour by the shipboard bore was likely to occur.

Susan stretched luxuriously and closed her eyes again, conscious of the sun shining outside the curtained porthole. She was in no hurry to get up—there was no hurry about anything for the next few days. No pressure of business, no deadlines, no emergencies—nothing could reach her here. What a lot people missed when they flogged themselves on and off jets, so fearful of wasting time, so unconscious of how to relax in the time they had saved.

She rolled over on one side and raised herself on an elbow, studying the printed list of available information beside the telephone. The weather: she dialled and discovered it was fair and sunny, the sea was calm, the temperature 63°F., the outlook good for tomorrow. Shipboard activities: what sounded like the same voice told her there would be a concert in the main lounge at 11:00 a.m., lifeboat drill at 3:00 p.m., a film in the cinema at 8:30 p.m., and cabaret in the night club from 10:00 p.m. until 2:00

a.m. The time: the ubiquitous voice let her know that when she heard the chime the time would be 8:45 precisely.

The daily news bulletin (in English): here, at last, was a different voice, in the accents of the country rapidly retreating beyond the horizon: ". . . The UN Security Council will meet today to decide . . ."

Susan reclined against the pillow. How often had she heard that voice as an accompaniment to breakfast in the Manhattan flat she shared with Betty and Jean? For a moment, she was back there. As the voice droned on with the international news, Betty would come dashing from the bathroom to gulp a glass of orange juice standing beside the fridge. Jean would be buttering toast and pouring coffee. She herself—

The ship gave a brief juddering lurch as an unexpectedly large wave slapped it broadside. Susan opened her eyes. It would not be happening at this hour, of course. This was the 7:30 a.m. news report, recorded from a local New York station, to play endlessly for the information of interested passengers until replaced by a 6:00 p.m. report in the evening. This voice would follow them across the Atlantic, at least until the half-way point, when it would be easier for the ship's radio to pick up the BBC news bulletins, and these would replace the New York newscasts.

The voice changed slightly, shading into a more concerned tone as it came to the local news. Then it read the catalogue of murders, robberies, rapes, arson and mugging—those that people had bothered to report. The grim total of a night's carnage in a beleaguered city. The city that had held so much promise and so much menace, that had begun so proudly. *Thine alabaster cities gleam* . . .

Susan replaced the receiver and stood up, games with the telephone ended by the intrusion of too much reality. She rang for the steward and ordered tea and toast, then ran her bath.

Accustomed by now to the low, shallow American tubs, she watched bemused as the tub filled. The Brides in the Bath murders, she realized now, could only have been European. These narrow deep tubs were made to order for nefarious purposes—they were also more satisfying and re-laxing, once one got into them safely.

There was a tap on her stateroom door and she called out in answer. She had no answering reply but, when she looked into the stateroom, her breakfast tray was on the bedside table. She turned off the water and went into the stateroom, settling herself in the armchair on the other side of the table and pouring a cup of tea.

You could see how smooth the ocean was by the way the tea barely moved in the cup. Only a faint gentle swell on the surface emulated the deeper swell beneath the hull of the ship. They'd be very lucky if the weather held like this for the whole crossing.

The toast, swaddled in a linen napkin and nestled in-side the aluminium covered receptacle, was hot and crisp. The jam was blackcurrent—seen so rarely on New York ta-bles as to be a luxury.

The tea—she lifted the lid and looked into the pot—was from a teabag. She replaced the lid with a faint sigh. One couldn't have everything.

Nevertheless, one was closer to having everything on the *Beatrice Cenci* than one had been for a long time. She felt tiny, unnoticed nerves begin to loosen and unwind. Deny it though she always did, there was strain involved in living in any large city. And life in New York had an under-lying tension which was unknown in European cities since the days of footpads and highwaymen. When every cocktail party, every gathering of friends produced a new story of assault, of robbery, of narrow escapes, it was no wonder that New York faces were taut and strained, New York eyes alert and suspicious. And yet one grew used to it, as one could grow accustomed to anything. It was only when you got away from it, outside the city for a few days, that you began to realize just how harrowing the tension had been.

She finished the toast, poured another cup of tea and carried it into the bathroom, balancing it carefully as she stepped into the tub. Favouring her scarred leg, she sub-sided into the bath and leaned back, sipping her tea. A few more nerves unwound.

"PROVIDED ALWAYS . . ." That had been an additional source of anxiety during the last few weeks in New York. An extra reason for crossing streets with extra care, for avoiding dark corners, for turning abruptly into a shop if the same person had been walking behind her for too many blocks.

Melodramatic? Perhaps, but . . . She glanced down at her mangled leg. Once again, Eric's face rose in her memory as it had looked on that day: frightened, but exultant. *("You're all right, Susan. You're alive. Don't cry, Susan. They're only going to shoot Thunderbolt—they're not going to shoot you, Susan.")* In those moments, she had suddenly become as precocious as he was, hearing the regret in his voice, seeing the world briefly through his eyes. Without her, the daughter of the house, all of this would belong to him some day: the estate, the stud farm, the investments, the city freeholds. *("You're all right, Susan, you're still alive.")*

And going to stay alive. Alive to claim every last one of her rights. Oh, Eric could continue to run the stud farm, he loved it and he'd been making a very good job of it—but *she* would own it. There might be problems with Eric, but she would face those later. After the three-month period was safely past, after everything was safely hers.

She drained the cup and leaned over the edge of the tub with it. The floor seemed to rise up to meet it, but not quite enough. There was a clatter as the cup and saucer dropped the last couple of inches she couldn't reach. It didn't matter.

She leaned back in the hot relaxing water and stretched luxuriously. The running was over and she had reached sanctuary. Here, on the *Beatrice Cenci*, there was nothing to worry about. No cars that might career around a corner out of control; no muggers who might decide to cut a throat because a purse had not held as much money as they hoped, or just for kicks; none of the thousand dangers that lurked in the concrete jungle of the city.

She could afford to relax, to drop her guard. For these next few days she was as safe as anyone could be anywhere in the world.

Chapter 5

"Lifeboat drill in half an hour, Mrs. Abercrombie." It would be too much for her so soon, of course, but the pretence must be kept up. "Do you want to—?"

"No, no, no." Mrs. Abercrombie made the familiar, brushing-away motion with her hands. "You go, find out what lifeboat we're supposed to be in, and—" she grinned mirthlessly— "if the ship starts to sink, abandon me and get there yourself. I'd never make it."

Val laughed lightly, wondering if it were as much of a joke as Mrs. Abercrombie intended. "The *Beatrice Cenci* won't sink. She may not be the biggest liner afloat, but she's the newest, and she has the last word in safety equipment, stabilizers—"

"That was what they said about the *Titanic*." Mrs. Abercrombie glanced at her wryly. "It always seems to me to be tempting Providence to put out publicity like that. It's seemed so to most of the steamship lines ever since. I notice they've avoided extravagant claims like the plague— until now. Of course—" she shrugged— "the Italians—"

"Now, Mrs. Abercrombie, that isn't fair," Val said. "The Italians have always been great mariners. Christopher Columbus discovered America—"

"And a lot of people have wished he'd left well enough alone ever since. No—" She cut off any intended protest. "I know."

"All right," Val said quickly. Perhaps it had started as a joke, but Mrs. Abercrombie was growing pinched and white about the lips. The joke was too close to home, bringing with it the realization of her own helplessness in the face of any real crisis which might arise. It was not easy for a person who had

31

been vital and active to know that she was now forced to be dependent on other people in an emergency.

"Why don't you lie down for a while?" Val suggested. "I'll come straight back after lifeboat drill and take you up on deck. Unless you'd like to go up now——?"

"No, no," Mrs. Abercrombie said. "There'll be too much noise, too much confusion, too many people rushing around not knowing where they're going. I'd just be in the way."

"Later then," Val said. Too many witnesses to Mrs. Abercrombie's weakness was what Mrs. Abercrombie really meant. It was bad enough that the minimal number of First Class passengers should see her in her detested wheelchair, but passengers from Tourist would be converging upon the lifeboats on the uppermost deck—and making the most of their sole opportunity to take a good look around the First Class quarters. "You'll lie down here for a while?"

"Very well," Mrs. Abercrombie agreed. Still tight-lipped, she allowed Valerie to help her back to her bunk, but insisted on lying on top, rather than getting under the covers.

"Don't fuss so!" she said. "I'm perfectly all right. Go and find your life-jacket—you'll need it for the boat drill. That's as much as they ever do—tell you you've fastened it on the wrong way, and re-tie it so fast you can't see what they've done."

"I think I saw the life-jackets in the locker in the bathroom . . ." Val escaped gratefully to her own stateroom.

She sank down into the comfortable armchair, pulling the wireless message from her pocket, still in no hurry to open it and read whatever further vindictiveness Ralphie had thought up for his parting shot. This would be his final chance. Back in London, in her home territory, she could vanish without trace. He would not be able to find her again, to exact any more revenge.

The thought buoyed her enough to allow her to open the envelope. The message inside was so unexpected it came as a jolt to her.

BON VOYAGE. HAVE ORDERED TWO BOTTLES
CHAMPAGNE FOR YOUR TABLE LAST NIGHT OUT.
SEE THAT YOU GET IT. TAKE GOOD CARE OF AUNT
ALICIA. —MILDRED AND AUGUSTUS.

That was all it was. Mrs. Abercrombie's step-niece and
nephew demonstrating that they were properly devoted.
And, incidentally, making sure that they got their money's
worth, that the champagne ordered and paid for would actually be delivered. Somewhere else aboard this ship, she
supposed, a steward or stewardess had been well tipped to
keep an eye on Nurse Meadows and make certain that Mrs.
Abercrombie was being well looked after and not neglected
in any way.

Mildred and Augustus would always insist on their
money's worth—and more if they could get it. She had
known that the instant she met them.

It had been a spur-of-the-moment impulse to answer
that advertisement. Her third night in New York City, already with the feeling of being imprisoned in a city where a
woman alone might be risking more than she cared to lose if
she moved about after dark without either a male escort or
female companion, Val had sat alone in her hotel room reduced to the Help Wanted columns of her newspaper, having read everything else.

The advertisement had caught her eye, holding out the
promise of a trip to Europe—which suddenly appealed
more to her than staying on in New York alone—and the
telephone number had been included. Spontaneously, she
had found herself reaching out for her own telephone.

There had been a brief verbal tussle with a servant,
then a voice so cold and wintry that her own voice in response, in defence, projected the icy crystalline of English
at its most chilling. It had interested Augustus, though; she
was granted an interview.

Protective coloration. She had not realized until she
donned it again how deeply she had missed her uniform.
And, had she been deliberately scheming, it would have

been the cleverest move she could have made. The approving nod of Augustus's head as he studied her, told her that.

"Ah, yes." Augustus's sigh was one of relief, perhaps gratification. "Yes, I think you'll do nicely."

Val lowered her lashes. The past few months had left her with few illusions. Her English accent counted for a great deal in snob value, she knew, but even more importantly, it signalled that she would be satisfied with a one-way passage. If Augustus were to employ an American nurse, he would have to guarantee her return fare.

"You'll be going First Class, you know." He seemed anxious to impress the honour upon her, although she suspected that inwardly he was mourning the lost world where a servant would travel on one of the lower decks. "First Class—in fact, a suite. We have insisted that Aunt Alicia must pamper herself in every way. She's been very ill—she had us badly frightened."

"Of course," Val agreed sympathetically. She had already been taken to meet—to be approved by—Mrs. Abercrombie. The signs of a sharp and precipitous illness had been there in her face to be read, the wan but determined smile with which she welcomed Val a signal that the worst was over.

"Mildred—" He glanced at his sister, his expression warming slightly. "Mildred cared for her night and day. She spared no effort to pull Aunt Alicia through."

Scarcely surprising, then, that Mildred should now look so nerve-ridden and haggard. Intensive nursing, even for those trained to it, could take a surprising toll.

"It was originally intended that Mildred should accompany Aunt Alicia on this trip, but—" he looked at his sister and looked away again— "Mildred needs a rest herself now. It would be too much to expect—"

Even now, Val could not recall Mildred's face clearly, but Mildred's hands haunted her. Hands endlessly twisting and twining upon each other. Fingers returning to a plain gold ring, pulling it up past the joint of the third finger of the left hand as though she would take it off and hurl it from her, and then savagely jamming it back down as far as it would go. Over and over again, while Mildred's eyes stared unseeingly into space.

At one point, the telephone had rung. It had been the only time that Mildred had shown any sign of animation— or even of being aware of her surroundings.

"Let the maid answer it!" Augustus's curt command had dropped Mildred back into her chair like a broken doll. "We don't want any more unpleasantness. Do we?"

"No. No." Mildred's right hand sought out her left again, the gold ring twirled, moved upwards, hesitated, slammed down again. "No. You're right, Augustus. You're always right."

Augustus accepted the tribute with a self-satisfied little nod, then turned to Val, frowning slightly, as though wondering whether or not the brief, intense scene needed any explanation—or justification. Perhaps what he had seen in her face decided him.

"My sister," he said, "has had an additional problem— as if Aunt Alicia's illness weren't quite enough for us to cope with. Mildred—" He glanced anxiously at her again, but Mildred was unseeing, her ears attuned only to the low-voiced conversation taking place at the telephone in the hall.

"Mildred—" his lips pursed in distaste—"Mildred made an unfortunate marriage. Oh, I warned her the man was nothing but a fortune-hunter—"

For a brief moment, Val's heart went out to Mildred, but Augustus was still speaking. Evidently he did not feel any response was called for from one who was, essentially, a servant.

"But she wouldn't listen. Now, of course, the inevitable is taking place. A divorce—a most acrimonious divorce." Augustus's hands made that brushing-away gesture she was to become so familiar with.

"It's an additional reason why Mildred cannot accompany Aunt Alicia at this time. We have discovered that her—" he could hardly bear to say the word— "her husband—has been planning to take advantage of her absence from this country to introduce a most spiteful and unnecessary note into the court proceedings. He cannot be allowed to get away with such a thing."

"I see," Val murmured in vague partisanship.

"Ah, yes." Satisfaction tinged Augustus's voice. "That creature will arrive in court with his lies, believing Mildred safely out of the way on the high seas. And then he'll see her across the courtroom with her lawyer, filing a cross-petition. Ah, yes. He'll learn he isn't so smart."

Mildred's hands twisted, stilled, and began to writhe again.

"Well," Augustus said briskly, seeming to have disposed of that matter to his satisfaction and concentrating on Val once more. "I think the most satisfactory thing for you to do would be to move in here for the week until the ship sails, don't you? That way, you can get accustomed to Aunt Alicia's routine and take some of the burden off Mildred."

"That will be all right," Val agreed. She found she was pleased at the idea of leaving her lonely hotel room, of becoming part of a household again. There was just one more thing—rather a chance, but it might be noticed if she acted out of character.

"If you want references—" she offered.

"I don't think that will be necessary." Augustus gave a wintry smile. "I flatter myself that I'm an excellent judge of people."

Apart from which, there would not really be time for him to send and receive letters. Which was as well. He might be rather amazed at the answers he would get. Val smiled back demurely.

"In any case," Augustus said, "you'll basically be on duty for only a short time. Aunt Alicia will be staying with friends in Mentone and they'll see to her. And Mildred—" He glanced at his sister uneasily, but she still was paying no attention. "Mildred," he went on more firmly, "will fly over and return with Aunt Alicia in the spring. In fact, I may send her over earlier—once the divorce is out of the way— so that she can have a few weeks herself to recuperate. However, that can be decided later." He smiled again.

"The main thing is, thanks to you, we now have Aunt

Alicia taken care of. With her settled, I can devote myself to Mildred's concerns." He nodded.

"Yes, despite this necessary last-minute change in our arrangements, I shall see that Mildred isn't cheated out of her little trip abroad."

Nothing to do with her own past life at all, nothing to do with Ralphie. The agitation leading up to opening the message had just been her persecution complex working overtime again.

Except that it was more than a complex. Those last few days in the mid-West *had* been full of persecution. So much so that the scars would remain for a long, long time. Perhaps for the rest of her life.

Even just the day before yesterday, she had thought she'd seen Ralphie walking down Lexington Avenue ahead of her. It could not have been Ralphie, of course. Her common sense had told her that. He was just a type—there were millions of American men built to that same tall solid frame, with dark blond hair achieving a compromise between a fashionable length and a "respectable" hair style. Ralphie had been ordinary—so ordinary that she ached sometimes to remember just what it had been she had first seen in him. As though, if she could remember that, it might restore something to her that she had lost—or forgotten.

Yet, even while her common sense had tried to over-rule her emotions, her feet had carried her forward, trying to catch up with him, to walk past and take a good look, to see if—

He had reached the corner ahead of her, just making the traffic lights for pedestrians. By the time she got there, the lights had turned against her, a solid stream of traffic flowing past made it impossible to cross the street. A couple of over-sized delivery vans blocked her view for moments at a time. When she could see across the street again, when the traffic signal was clear for her to cross, he had disappeared.

Marian Babson

It could not have been Ralphie, in any case. What would he have been doing in New York?

Bundled up in his miniature life-jacket, a solid, bulky chunk from chin to belly button, Guido looked like a tiny football player. All that was missing was the helmet.

"*'You've got to be a football hero—,'*" Gloria hummed as she fastened the white tapes.

Guido chuckled. He was finding travel one great big laugh all the way.

"*There* you are!" She finished him off with a big gift-wrap rosette and there was still plenty of tape left. It took away from the football image a bit, but gave him such a jaunty look that she had to laugh. Besides, it was practically her trade mark. The gift-wrap rosette on all her packages, betokening just that little extra bit of care and attention, had been one of the things that had got her business off to such a flying start. That, and the best quality, absolutely unique merchandise she had uncovered on her spare-no-pains buying trips around the world. The best quality at the lowest price, and the customer could always be certain of old-fashioned service and personal attention. It worked. Just look where it had got her today.

First Class on the *Beatrice Cenci*.

She was going to have to admit it when she wrote to Lorenzo tonight: there *was* something special about First Class. Especially on this ship.

Later today, she wanted to investigate the Gift Galleries amidship. She had just got a glimpse of them after breakfast, too early for the shops to be open, but everyone was already milling around window-shopping. The Gift Galleries were already famous both ashore and afloat.

"Far more than just a duty-free shopping centre, the *Beatrice Cenci* Gift Galleries are a permanent floating display of the finest of modern Italian craftsmanship, there to be explored at your leisure during the voyage."

That was what the travel brochure had promised, and the *Beatrice Cenci* was delivering.

Already it had given her an idea. All those beautiful

38

shops, filled with all those luxury goods—and all Italian. All one-sided. Everything from the *Beatrice Cenci*'s home port and nothing representing the country to which she made most of her voyages. Was that fair? Was it even sensible?

What about all those returning Italian passengers who had had their time in the States completely monopolized by affectionate relatives, leaving them no time to shop for the remembrances they must bring back to friends? Even those who found time for shopping always forgot someone, and then there were the little last-minute items, the impulse buys—Gloria knew all about those. Such customers must find it too late when they got on board ship and began remembering the others to whom they should be bringing presents. And presents that were American, not some trifle purchased in the Gift Galleries—Italian and an admission of defeat, a clear implication that the loved ones had been forgotten on shore and only remembered at the last minute aboard ship.

So, why not? Oh, perhaps not a full-scale Gloria Grandi Speciality Shoppe in the Gift Galleries—not yet. But, for a start, why shouldn't one of the shops carry a few Gloria Grandi Special Products? Just a few items that were uniquely American and yet in keeping with the range of Italian goods on offer.

Let's see . . . Oblivious of Guido, of everything, she got into her life-jacket automatically, lost in making out her mental list.

The Knickerbocker Selection—that always went well. One of the best items in her line and absolutely delicious. Home-made, hand-dipped chocolates, made by a group of housewives in Schenectady who had banded themselves together into a cottage industry and were always inundated with more orders than they could reasonably fill without dropping the quality of their product.

She frowned. Putting them on to the *Beatrice Cenci* would reduce the quota available for her own shop. And yet, it would be worth it, in publicity terms alone, to have the Gloria Grandi name represented in the Gift Galleries.

And Indian jewellery. Some of the Navajo silver-and-turquoise bracelets, belts, necklaces and ear-rings. Also some of the best beadwork—were they doing it out along the Mohawk and Taconic Trail? She'd have to check. It would make a marvellous subsidiary label, sounding both American and exotic at the same time.

And how about—?

Alarm bells clamoured wildly, jerking her back to earth.

Guido gulped a great breath and began to bellow, frightened and outraged by all the noise. This was a development he didn't like at all.

"Oh, baby—" Gloria swooped on him. "You've got a great track record—don't spoil it now."

She picked him up. Their life-jackets clunked together awkwardly. Guido gave her a watery smile and reached out to explore the strange orange objects that kept so much distance between them.

"That's better, baby," Gloria encouraged. "You don't want to cry now. We've got to go up on deck now. In front of all those people. You don't want them to see you crying, do you? You're getting to be such a big boy now—"

She broke off abruptly as Guido gave her a strangely accusing look—as though he knew that, for those few minutes while she had been concentrating on business, she had forgotten him completely. It was Lorenzo's look, too, when he sensed he was out of her thoughts, "just a second fiddle" to the Shoppe.

It was just some sort of physiological trick, of course, the way they said it was only wind when very tiny babies seemed to smile at you, but Guido even seemed to look older.

Perhaps this was at the core of Lorenzo's feelings: this knowledge that this was the way life slipped by. While you were doing your best—thinking about work, the way you had to if you wanted to get ahead—you were missing some of the other things along the way. The things most women thought of as the best things.

And yet, the Shoppe *was* one of the best things—for her. Did that have to mean that she was lacking something as a woman? Because she could get so much enjoyment out of pulling off a good business deal? Wasn't that what men did—and were they considered less male because of that? Except that, in so many cases, they excused themselves that they were doing it all for the wife and kids.

Well, she'd started the Shoppe—and become a success—before she had a kid. Before Lorenzo, too. Was she supposed to go around apologizing to him for that? How did she know that he'd even have paid that much attention to some little mouse who'd never been anywhere or done anything? Sure, she knew that part of it had been that he'd wanted an American wife so that he could get to the States. She'd known it on that Italian visit when her relatives had arranged their meeting—known, too, that the relatives were trying to make a match for their over-age American cousin. She'd gone along for the laughs—but the laugh had been on her. Maybe it still was. Even with Guido and the memories of all the happy times—between fights—she couldn't quite forget the way it had begun. Because Lorenzo had needed an American wife. But the fact that a successful woman with plenty of money had fallen for him was a bonus, wasn't it? And did she go around asking him if he'd have loved her if she'd been a penniless nobody?

No! Certainly not! She didn't even ask herself that.

The bells were still clanging. She ought to go and find their lifeboat station. Not that there would ever be any danger on a ship like the *Beatrice Cenci*, but it was part of being a good citizen to obey the rules and to involve yourself in community exercises like this. And she had to set a good example to Guido. No matter how young he was, there was no way of knowing how much a kid was taking in.

She scanned Guido's face anxiously. Reassuringly, it was a blobby, good-natured baby's face again. He grinned at her, blowing a saliva bubble, as he had done long months ago when far more of a baby.

Yet, beneath the baby mask, the other masks poised, waiting their turn: the schoolboy, the adolescent, the teenager, the football player. All of them were there: waiting, ready to rush on stage far too soon. She saw herself waiting

41

at home while he was out on the football field, hoping he'd come home in one piece, without broken bones, without—

Who was she kidding? The big football games took place on Saturday afternoons. The busiest time at the Shoppe. *That* was where she'd be on a Saturday afternoon—every Saturday afternoon. Well, maybe, if it was a *very* important game. But—

"Oh, baby, baby—" She hugged him impulsively, convulsively. "Don't grow up too soon."

Lifeboat Station No. 3.

Life-jacket draped as negligently as she could arrange it over her arm, Susan lounged within comfortable strolling distance of Lifeboat Station No. 3. It was just one of the many subterfuges she had grown adept at during her life as a semi-cripple.

This way, there was no pushing, no crowding, no question of being caught up in the pseudo-semi-hysterical panic that engulfed so many travellers as they thought, *"Suppose it was for real?"*

The ones accustomed to air travel, to fastening their seat belts and consigning their souls to whatever God they believed in, with the comforting knowledge that there was nothing more whatever that they could do—they were the ones most prone to panic as the realization dawned on them that, aboard ship, everything depended upon them and what they could do. There was no lying back passively. They had to get on life-jackets, dress warmly in case of prolonged exposure, get to the lifeboat station, wait to be loaded aboard, help with the lowering of the lifeboats, think about the practicalities of hitting the ocean surface without swamping, rowing away from the undertow of a powerful ship going under, keeping afloat, remaining in the main sea channels, signalling for help, apportioning rations if that help was too long in finding them, keeping up morale in the face of growing discouragement, thirst, hunger, fear.

It was no wonder that, in this age of the voyeur, the armchair traveller, the fatalist, so many preferred going by air. It was not solely that the airplane was cheaper and faster, it was that the die was quickly cast, the decision swift and final. For good or ill, it was all over in a matter of moments, with no effort called for from themselves. It was the complete casting of one's burdens—of life itself—on to the shoulders of another. It was, perhaps, the substitution of a High Priest—the pilot—for a God so many could no longer believe in. With the votive offering—the coins in the slot for the insurance to assuage the grief of those left behind, to assure them that they had been considered, right up to the last.

Air was for the defeatists, water for the fighters. Both were elements but, with water under you, you were sustained, held up—for how long might depend on you. That was the decision too many could not face, wanted to have made for them. But they would not be travelling on board the *Beatrice Cenci* in the first place.

And what of her? Susan swung away from the railing as the alarm bells started. What if there were a real emergency? She would not be conveniently loitering near her lifeboat station with her life-jacket over her arm. Trouble could happen at any time, it didn't take the convenience of the passengers into consideration. Nor did the best-laid plans of the authorities in case of emergency always work out as intended.

She thought of those terrible stories about the *Titanic*. Of the forgotten Steerage passengers, trustingly fighting their way through to their own lifeboat stations below decks, waiting hopefully for the solid steel bulwarks to be dropped so that they could clamber out into their lifeboats, which would have been lowered to their level partially filled with First Class passengers, and were supposed to be waiting for them. Waiting, for the solid steel walls to slide away, waiting . . . not knowing the panic that was spreading above decks, the confusion that was sweeping away all plans, all intelligence. Waiting . . . for the help that never came. Receiving, instead, the icy embrace of the North Atlantic as it gurgled through the tilting, shifting ship, drawing it down into the depths from which there was no escape, no return.

"Women and children first!" The light-hearted cry seemed to explode in her ear. She looked up to see him bowing her past—the archetypal American businessman. Slightly grizzled, with a twinkle in his eyes, mocking her urgency, reminding her that it was all make-believe, that this was one of the newest, steadiest ships afloat, that nothing was going to go wrong.

She smiled back at him—she couldn't help it. And then she had swung beyond him to Lifeboat Station No. 3.

When she looked back, he was still at Lifeboat Station No. 1, reaching out to take a young child while its mother caught her breath, twinkling at the mother now, instead of at her.

Just as well. He was probably the world's worst bore if one got to know him. It was only the ships that passed in the night which retained their mystery. And yet, she kept looking over her shoulder until the crowd of passengers from Tourist thronged between them, blotting out her view.

The public address system coughed into multi-lingual life. It welcomed them, it warned them, it exhorted them.

While it was going on, the officers moved up and down, inspecting their charges like indulgent Nannies. Straightening a life-jacket here, re-tying a tape there, patting a tempting cheek, pinching something even more tempting lower down, if they thought they could get away with it.

Susan held herself stiffly upright, expression coldly aloof, allowing for no margin of familiarity, no warmth of interest which would cool to the lukewarm discomfort of pity when she moved and the limp disclosed itself.

The officer hesitated in front of her, apologetically reached out and adjusted the mis-tied tapes, then stepped back and saluted briefly, passing on to the next passenger— a giggling teenager from Tourist—with obvious relief.

Why should she care? Her face remained frozen.

And yet, Women and Children First had seen her

limping. He must have, before he roared so merrily in her ear. It hadn't seemed to make any difference to him.

Why should it? He probably had some blue-rinsed, thoroughly spoiled wife waiting down below, too self-centred to join in anything so democratic as a lifeboat drill. All the nice ones had long since been tied to the leading strings of some ruthless bitch. Life had long ago taught her that.

Susan turned, involuntarily craning her neck. But she could see nothing. There were so many people, milling and massing, that it was impossible to distinguish any particular one.

Chapter 6

The ocean was high, the moon was full. The *Beatrice Cenci* danced blithely over the waves. She was young, she was trim, she was going home.

The farther out into the Atlantic she got, the more her own personality stirred and came to life. Out here, darting towards mid-Atlantic, she came into her own.

In dock, beside the older, more sedate liners, she looked flighty, possibly unreliable. Beside their smooth greyhound lines, she resembled an Afghan hound—her own sleek lines minimized, if not concealed, by the frippery disguising her. The flags fluttering atop, the Gift Galleries gleaming amidship, the frivolities of the staterooms, the gallantries of the crew, all combined to obliterate the realization that there was a well-planned, beautifully designed, solid working ship underneath.

People judged her by the surface, and she presented a beautifully polished surface. It did not matter that she gave the impression of having no solid worth. She knew, her crew knew, what lay beneath the surface. That was all that mattered.

Let the others—the uninitiated—put their money on the greyhounds. Let them discount the sleek lines beneath her fripperies.

Let them think of her as an Afghan hound, beautiful, useless, quite probably neurotic. She knew what she could do.

The *Beatrice Cenci* danced over the waves, heading for home.

No one dressed for dinner the first night out. Afterwards, Butler sought the bar and remained in it, one of the few diehards determined to keep the flag flying this first night out. After this he would be on duty, so to speak, and such indulgences would not be for him.

There were no women in the Borgia Bar tonight. He liked that. Not that he disapproved of women generally, or even women in bars. It was just that it was too much like work having them around.

Funny how many of his contracts had been women.

Not so odd, though, when you came to think of it. The sort of man who wanted his dirty work done for him tended to have qualms about killing in the first place. Which was why he ordered it done at one or two removes, didn't want to know any of the details, and preferred that it look like an accident. Probably, in more than a few of his cases, the customer had later managed to convince himself that it had been a genuine accident, that the accident he had ordered had not had time to occur, that a kindly fate had stepped in and ended an intolerable situation, leaving his conscience perfectly clear.

They never refused to pay the second half of the fee, though. Accidents could happen to anyone.

A woman hesitated in the doorway, staring into the bar. Butler tensed. If the woman had intended to enter, however, she seemed to have changed her mind. Perhaps she had been looking for someone. Or perhaps she had simply been doing a bit of exploring—and the Borgia Bar, done up as a Renaissance chapel, was one of the sights of the ship.

When the woman turned and disappeared from the doorway, Butler was not the only one who relaxed. More than he wished to be alone with their thoughts tonight. Shipboard was a great place for getting one's thoughts in order, deciding what one really thought about life and its problems. Conversely, it was also a great place for just switching off, letting the mind go blank. Women were a distraction to both states.

That was the trouble with women. If she'd come in, the whole atmosphere would have changed. Not that there was much atmosphere at the moment to change, but everyone would have been aware of her. Conversations—if there had been any conversations—would have become more guarded. Even if she had been rampant Women's Lib with a vocabulary like a fishwife, the men would still have watched their own language. The old customs die hard.

Don't knock it. That attitude was responsible for bringing him in a good income. That was why so many of his contracts were female.

The old taboos held even more strongly when it came to a female in a man's own family. The man was supposed to be the protector of the weak and vulnerable, the breadwinner, the provider of luxuries, the avenger of dishonour. His duty was to his wife, mother, daughter, sister, aunt, female cousins—to be the rock who could be clung to in time of peril.

It was unthinkable that he should be a source of peril himself. Even the customers didn't like to think about that one themselves. Never wanted to admit to their right hand what the left one was doing. Pretended that it was really nothing to do with them at all. They were innocent—the Butler did it. Personally, he had always done his best for . . . the deceased. Cosseted her, treated her with the kindness and respect due to her. It was unthinkable that any harm might have come to her through him. Why, she was a member of his own family. He'd *loved* her.

And yet, who could stand in a man's way better than a woman in his own family? Especially a woman who held the purse-strings. Nothing was more guaranteed to turn love to hate. The more quickly if the purse-strings weren't loosely, generously held. Even then, it wasn't the same as having all the money, with no restrictions, no questions to answer, no complaints, no one to say "No."

Some of them, of course, never did any more than just think about how nice it would be if . . . Others said "The hell with it" and stormed off and made their own way. Others waited for the inevitable, learning to toady and crawl as they waited, and tried not to think about how old they could be by the time the inevitable finally happened.

Others sent for Butler.

The smart ones, the impatient ones, the ones who kept an ear to the ground and knew how these things could be arranged.

Butler looked up and met a pair of female eyes so knowing that they startled him. Then he grinned and raised his goblet in the salute of one professional to another.

You saw a few off, too, in your time, cara.

The clear, glowing eyes of Lucrezia Borgia stared down at him. He hadn't noticed her up there over the bar like a stained-glass window. He'd been too busy keeping watch on what was happening around him—an occupational hazard. You could miss a lot that way. On the other hand, it could keep you alive so that you knew what you'd missed.

Farther along the bar, he saw a man staring at him, looking faintly shocked. Butler wiped the grin off his face, lest it seem welcoming. He was in no mood to talk. Not to a mutt like that.

He signalled for another drink, knowing it might be slightly unwise. He was already having dangerous thoughts. Like he'd like to talk to someone who could understand. How many of those were there around?

You knew the score, cara. His eyes went back to Lucrezia. Now, there was his kind of woman.

You, too, of course, sweetheart. Beatrice Cenci was right up there beside her. *But you had bad luck. Caught the first time you signed anyone off.* He shook his head, sketching a salute to her, too. It was the way the Big Boys had told him years back when he first joined the Syndicate—you had to have the luck. Nothing else counted, once the luck started running against you.

He hadn't spoken aloud, had he? The man at the far end of the bar was still looking faintly scandalized.

No, of course he hadn't. The first thing you learned in the Syndicate was to keep your mouth shut. Later, working as a freelance, it became even more important. It became part of an iron control that never slipped. What was biting the mutt then?

The fresh drink was set before him. Picking up the period goblet—you might almost call it a chalice, if your mind ran in that direction—and glancing upwards at the pseudo stained-glass windows, it clicked into place.

They weren't stained glass, of course, just some kind of coloured Perspex, but the effect—with some kind of lighting cleverly concealed behind them—was the same. Regardless of what they were made of, they were works of art. Modern artists had the right to work in any material they chose. And Lucrezia and Beatrice were works of art—no mistaking it. But he could see what was bothering the mutt.

The chalice, the stained-glass windows of ladies who definitely were no saints, the whole Renaissance chapel atmosphere. And Butler's own gesture in raising the chalice towards them. Perhaps it was no wonder the mutt was scandalized.

On the other hand, if he felt like that about it, why come into the Borgia Bar to begin with? He could have seen what it was like almost as soon as he had come through the arch and got his eyes accustomed to the darkness.

Don't blame the other guy, Butler. You've been careless. He had momentarily forgotten that there were always watching eyes—whether you noticed them or not. He'd have to be more careful in the future.

Even as he made the resolution, the other man abruptly rose and left the bar. Butler watched him go—there was an Espresso Coffee Bar a couple of decks below, that was more his line. Just the same, Butler ought to be more careful. It was the little things that started people wondering, gave you away in the end.

Butler shrugged and looked around surreptitiously. No one else was paying any attention. What the hell? Only a nut like that would think about it, put that kind of construction on the gesture. So what? Live dangerously.

Again Butler raised the goblet in salute. To Lucrezia, with admiration. To Beatrice, with sympathy.

And yet, you haven't done so badly, sweetheart. They've named a ship after you.

Butler chuckled. Would they ever name a ship after him? Possibly, possibly. Times changed, unfashionable points of view eventually became respectable.

He glanced upwards at the brooding Beatrice again. At the rate of centuries it took, though, it wouldn't be an ocean liner for him.

More likely a space ship. *Butler* to the stars. Yes, he liked that. He'd drink to that. He raised his goblet again: to the enchanting, the lethal, the understanding Lucrezia.

You saw a few off, too, in your time, cara.

Chapter 7

It was a great start to the second day at sea. She'd forgotten to set her watch ahead last night, Guido was fretting, and the cabin steward had seemed surly when she'd ordered late breakfast in her stateroom. Perhaps they should have gone by air, after all.

The weather didn't look so good, either. The sky was overcast, giving the impression of a lowering sun brooding behind the grey dreariness. The sea shimmered with white-tipped ripples, evidence of greater turbulence beneath the surface than there appeared to be at the moment. There was a solid wall of mist on the horizon—and they were sailing directly towards it.

She moved away from the porthole as the steward tapped perfunctorily at the door and brought in the breakfast tray. He glared at her with distaste, at Guido with gloomy suspicion. There was no doubt about it, he *was* surly. Probably expecting the baby to be sick the minute they hit a rough patch of sea.

Too bad—she tried not to smile, it could be misinterpreted by the steward as laughing at him—Lorenzo couldn't see this scene. Not even someone so determined as he to be jealous would be able to convince himself that the steward was quivering with lust for his irresistible wife.

"Signora!" He slammed down the tray and backed towards the door. "You wish anything else?" His tone defied her to be so presumptuous.

"Nothing more right now, thank you." She was aware, even before the tip of his nose twitched disdainfully, that she sounded like Lady Muck. She should have said something in Italian, something colloquial and matey.

On the other hand, why should she? She lifted her head as the door closed with an emphasis just short of a slam. Why ought she to curry favour with the help? She was paying enough for this trip—*and* he'd expect a tip at the end.

She shrugged. If he wanted to be in a bad temper, let him. He was nothing to her. If he didn't want to work with people, why didn't he go into a monastery? She didn't have to coax him into a good mood—she had enough of that with Lorenzo.

"No, baby—" She caught the chubby hand as it reached for the corner of the tray, threatening to overturn it.

Guido tried to pull away, beginning to whine. He was hungry, poor kid.

"Okay, come on." She sat down and gathered him into her lap, raising the orange juice to his lips. He gulped at it greedily, dribbling a bit down his chin and on to her sleeve. She'd have to set the travelling alarm clock tomorrow—remembering to turn it ahead first—breakfast was so much easier in the dining salon, where Guido could have a high chair.

More orange juice splashed on to her sleeve. Gloria gave an impatient exclamation then, just in time, realized that it wasn't Guido's fault. The ship had developed an erratic dipping motion. She looked up and across to the porthole in time to see the horizon blink into and out of sight.

Well, it was only to be expected, after all. They were quite a way out to sea now. Tomorrow they'd be halfway across—and this wasn't really the best time of the year to travel by sea. If it got no worse than this, they'd be lucky.

She reached for a piece of toast and tried to pour coffee while still steadying Guido's glass. Perhaps they'd just hit a rough patch of sea—the coffee swirled into the cup smoothly and settled there without further movement. Guido's orange juice met his lips and slipped back down the glass without splashing this time. Sometimes you did just hit a few rough waves now and then; it didn't necessarily mean that you were heading into dirty weather.

Guido pushed away the empty glass and burped contentedly before reaching for her toast.

"Wait a minute, baby." She evaded his clutching hand. "You don't want this. You like it with butter."

She had begun spreading butter on the toast, Guido watching her intently, when the thud came at the door. The steward? Back again with something he had forgotten?

"Come in," she called, but nothing happened. Perhaps his hands were full. She slid Guido to the floor and crossed to open the door.

There was no one there. At the far end of the corridor, one of the ship's officers hesitated and seemed to be at a loss to find himself in a dead end. He turned and made his way back slowly, nodding to her as he passed her open cabin door. Had he stumbled against it on his way down the corridor? And what was he doing here anyway, looking so lost? Didn't he know his way around his own ship?

"Signora," he mumbled, sketching a salute. The gold braid on his sleeve glittered.

"Good morning." Her smile was as perfunctory as his salute. She stepped back into the cabin quickly, closing the door against a sudden chill.

He had been one of the men in the Borgia Bar last night, she remembered. A shudder shook her as the strangeness of that moment she had paused in the doorway returned. Uncanny, the hostility she had felt radiating towards her from those men in the bar. None of them had been together, they were all sitting separately, so she wasn't interrupting a bull session or anything. Yet they had deliberately frozen her out, projecting a blank wall of defiance: defying her to enter, to disturb them from whatever private problems they were brooding over.

She had only wanted one little drink. Perhaps a bit of sociability. Guido was a darling, but he wasn't exactly a stimulating conversationalist—not for a few years yet.

But they had stopped her dead. She found herself unable to step into that bar, to intrude upon that solidly male preserve. Even Father Service had huddled over his drink, avoiding her eyes after that first brief shock of contact—like the others, willing her to go away and leave them alone.

So much for Joe and his "whooping it up" accusations. He should be on his own, lonesome, and looking for just a little human companionship after a hard day! It was always the ones who knew nothing about it who had the loudest mouths. Too bad he'd never be alone and—

Guido whimpered. His eyes were Lorenzo's again: accusing, injured, suspicious. She was off in her own world, forgetting his existence once more. And she had been so thrilled, so happy with him in the beginning.

"Yes, baby, I'm coming." She snatched up the toast, buttering it hastily. "I hadn't forgotten you. Not really. Not for one little minute."

Mrs. Abercrombie had passed a restless night. Too close to dawn, sleep had overtaken her. Those lost hours could not be regained and, when she woke, her head would be heavy for the rest of the day; she would be dazed and fretful, ready with complaints, uneasy without knowing why.

They had both slept through the breakfast hour and when Val woke, Mrs. Abercrombie still tossed in restless slumber. Yet she must be allowed to sleep for as long as she could, no matter how inadequate that sleep might be.

Valerie had not opened the curtains over the portholes. She had slipped out to the dining salon for a quick, unsatisfactory snack, spent mostly in fending off the Chief Steward's insistence that a hot and heavy luncheon must be despatched immediately to the Signora who was not feeling well. Val's determined thwarting of this idea had left him offended and gazing at her with thinly-veiled suspicion.

Quite probably, he was the one who had been suborned by Mildred and Augustus to watch over their step-aunt's welfare. Even now he was undoubtedly composing a libellous cablegram insinuating, if not accusing, that the reprehensible heartless nurse was attempting to starve the poor Signora Abercrombie to death. One must earn one's money—or at least appear to give value for it.

In the midst of her struggles to prevent the instant despatch of a tray to ruin Mrs. Abercrombie's brief slumber, Val had intercepted the kindly and amused eye of a fellow-passenger.

Now, stretched out in her deck-chair, she looked up to find that same fellow-passenger hovering above her.

"That steward sounded pretty determined," the man said, twinkling navy blue eyes at her. "Why didn't you give up and let him do what he wanted?"

"Because it would have been extremely bad for my patient." Valerie was aware of the primness of her reply, but could not recall the words. She was sheltering, as she had so often during these past months, behind her uniform, behind the expected image of a professional nurse. Would she ever have the courage to come out into the open, to be herself again?

"She's a game old girl, travelling in a wheelchair." He didn't seem daunted. Coolly, he pre-empted the empty deck-chair beside her. "What's the matter with her?"

"Nothing very much." She would not discuss her patient, particularly with people who wanted to gossip.

"Oh." He nodded wisely. "A hypochrondriac, huh?" He was a retired manufacturer, she had heard, and perhaps well versed in the ways of malingering on both shop floor and executive levels.

"Certainly not! Mrs. Abercrombie has been quite ill, but she's much better now. In fact, she's making a splendid recovery."

"I see." Disconcertingly, he looked as though he might not be seeing the same thing she was. His eyes surveyed her face thoughtfully—as though he might be about to recognize a likeness, remember something.

Instinctively, her hand moved up to shield her face in the gesture that had become automatic during the nightmare days and nights when she had been besieged by press and cameramen. She caught the gesture in time and turned it into a brushing back of her hair. She could not spend the rest of her life hiding. It was time to begin coming out into the open again. She was innocent—it was only the pressure of circumstances, the attitudes of other people, that had forced her into feeling—and acting—like a criminal. She had nothing to be ashamed of.

"This your first crossing? I mean—" his little nod indicated that he had noted her accent— "did you come over by ship or did you fly?"

"We went by ship." And that had been the beginning of it all. "I was attending a patient. An American who was taken ill on holiday. Doctor considered that the sea voyage home would be better for him."

"That's right." This time, his nod registered approval. "Nothing like a ship, is there?"

He was leaning back in Mrs. Abercrombie's deck-chair, obviously all ready to settle in for the afternoon. In the deck-chair on the other side of him, a youngish man had abandoned his magazine by unobtrusive stages and was now openly awaiting an opportunity to join in the conversation. It was the sort of situation she had been hoping to avoid. She did not want to be drawn into any semblance of shipboard life.

"You had the right idea." He was still approving, although as he squinted his eyes against the sun which suddenly broke through the overcast, there was something in them which might have been a measuring look. "Take up nursing—see the world. With your fare paid all the way. If I'd had a daughter, that would have been the advice I'd have given her. You never have to worry with a profession like that behind you."

The youngish man dropped his magazine on the deck and leaned forward to retrieve it. Perhaps it was just a coincidence that the action would give him a better view of her, but Val's hand went towards her face again and this time she let it, raising it as though to shield her eyes, but effectively blocking off most of her expression.

"Sun is bright, all of a sudden, isn't it?" The manufacturer glanced skywards. "Weather's decided to improve, after all."

The *Beatrice Cenci* dipped suddenly into the trough of a wave, sending the magazine the youngish man was groping for skittering down the deck to rest under Val's deck-chair. At the far end of the deck there was a clatter of crockery as cups and saucers on the trolley about to dispense afternoon tea jarred against each other uneasily.

"It's okay, I'll get it, fella." The manufacturer began to reach beneath her deck-chair for the magazine.

Shipboard convention demanded that she shift in her chair, making helpful noises, and try to look concerned. She lay still and closed her eyes, willing them both to go away and leave her in peace.

"Now, you take me—" From the rustling noises, he had retrieved the magazine successfully and returned it to its owner. There had been a murmur of thanks and a "Not at all" sort of reply. Val firmly kept her eyes closed, but the older man's attention had returned to her nonetheless.

"Now, you take me—" he continued, blithely ignoring the fact that everything about her attitude was signalling that she had no intention of taking him, would not have had him as a gift, and only wished that he would go away and bore someone else.

"Me," he continued, "I broke my neck all my life chasing a buck. Lots of things I wanted to do, I said to my wife, 'Wait till I've retired—then we'll do some fast catching up.' Only—" he sighed— "it didn't work that way."

Val kept her eyes closed against the unwanted revelation about to be thrust on her. Nevertheless, she was still aware of the youngish man in the deck-chair beyond, poised to enter the conversation at the first opening.

"She died—" he went on to the inevitable point, over-riding the condoling murmur in their throats— "suddenly. With no warning. Not that I'd have had it otherwise—but, if she'd had something lingering, something slower—Not in pain—but there's so much you can do with drugs these days. We could still have seen something of the world together—if we'd had time . . ."

Val murmured again, and heard the other man begin to speak. Good. He'd been longing to join in the conversation.

Let him work his passage. Better yet, let them start talking to each other and she could slip away and leave them.

". . . myself." Formalities over, the youngish man was launching upon his own potted biography. "Looked forward to this for years . . . always been my subject . . ."

Val opened her eyes unwillingly and turned her head. But he wasn't watching her, he was staring up at the seagulls wheeling overhead, saying his piece as mechanically as though he had said it too often—or learned it by rote.

". . . saving up. I'll probably do this only once in my life, so I decided to do it First Class all the way."

"That's right," the manufacturer approved. "That's the spirit. Do these things while you're still young. Well," he amended, with another, harder look at the other man's face, "young enough."

"Precisely . . ." The colourless, slightly pedantic voice went on relentlessly, as though he might forget his speech if he allowed interruptions from the class. ". . . Sabbatical year. Not my turn, strictly speaking, but no one else particularly wanted this year and I did. They were very lenient, particularly when I mentioned my thesis. The prospect of another Doctorate in the Faculty credits appealed to them."

"Learning's another thing I never had enough of," the elder man said. "Another thing there was never enough time for. But I'm not against it—" He was anxiously assuring, as though Learning could live or die according to his judgement of it. "I'm all for it. Especially for younger people, especially the way things are these days—new technologies and everything. You can't know too much these days."

"You may think that there's nothing left to be said about the Renaissance," the professor riposted, quite as though they were talking about the same subject. "However, I *do* feel that there are still a number of valid observations and criticisms to be made—"

"You take me, I knew enough for my own time—but my time is over now, I admit it. I've had it pretty good, though. I started out from nothing and built up my own factory, branched out a little—not too much—never get so overextended you can't pull back in time and ride a recession. That's the secret of making a go of manufacturing—"

They were talking together amiably now. Rather, each was absorbed in his own monologue. Neither was paying any attention to her, it was her chance to get away.

Val slid forward in the deck-chair, cautiously swinging her legs to one side, trying to be unobtrusive about it. She wanted to remain forgotten, to be on her feet and on her way before either of them could realize it and make a move to stop her, to draw her back into the conversation again.

"Hey—" Too late. The manufacturer had turned, staring at her with consternation. She was caught halfway out of the deck-chair, hoisting herself with desperate determination up and around the wooden arms.

"Hey there, little lady—you're not running out on us, are you?"

"My patient," Val offered quickly. "I really must go and look in on my patient."

"Oh, sure." The man sank back into his deck-chair. "I keep forgetting you're on duty. I guess your time isn't really your own."

"It isn't," Val agreed, grateful for the straw from which she could build future bricks of resistance when drinks or meetings were suggested.

"Oh?" A vague dissatisfaction shadowed the professor's face as he turned towards her. "I'd, er . . . thought we might go down and have a drink before dinner . . . all of us. The Borgia Bar is quite amusing. Have you seen it?"

"I just glanced in last night," she admitted. "While I was exploring the ship. I got the impression that it was an all-male preserve."

"I know what you mean," the manufacturer said. "I wasn't in there ten minutes before I started looking around for the sign. I figured it must have said 'Men Only' somewhere around, but it must just have been one of those things that happen every once in a while. Ladies all felt like an early night after their first day at sea, I guess."

She had gained her feet, refolded the blanket and replaced it at the foot of her deck-chair. She took a small step backward, then another, ready to turn and go.

"That's right." Something in his voice halted her, his face was bland and blank. "Run along and take good care of your patient. You never know with these old dames—maybe she'll leave you something in her will and then you won't have to work any more."

"That's a thought." She kept her voice even, but turned and moved away swiftly so that he might not see her face flame and know that he had struck home. Had it just been an accidental remark, the random heavy-handed pleasantry his sort indulged in? Or had there been deliberate malice behind it? Was it his way of letting her know that he had recognized her, that he "had her number"?

She would stay in the suite this evening, she decided. Play cards, perhaps, with Mrs. Abercrombie. And, for the rest of the voyage, she would do her best to avoid her shipmates.

"Italian comedy—English sub-titles," the schedule of activities had announced on the bulletin board outside the main lounge. Susan turned away thoughtfully. She had never heard of the film, but the only alternative the evening offered was Bingo in the card room, so she might as well go to the film. There was an hour to kill before it started, though.

Perhaps a couple of turns around the deck. She swung open the heavy door and stepped carefully over the high sill. She was unprepared for the gust of wind that struck her—it had been quite still just before dinner.

Determinedly, she moved away from the shelter of the doorway. It hadn't started to rain yet, but the threat was there in the dampness of the wind. The deck was already slippery underfoot, slick with the moisture of the heavy mist beginning to envelop the ship.

It's going to be a rough night, she thought, and felt the deck tilt beneath her feet as though in agreement.

She caught her balance awkwardly, glad that the weather had driven possible witnesses inside, aware that her limp was worsening. Once she had loved the rain, in the long-ago days before her own leg became a thing of treachery, weaker than the rest of her slight wiry body, susceptible to rain, ready to ache with the first onset of dampness, apt to buckle under her and spill her ignominiously on the floor of buses and trains at an unexpected lurch.

One learned to fall so that the sudden spills brought less pain than embarrassment. The rush of onlookers to help her to her feet, the anxious enquiries, were more devastating than the occasional scraped knee or laddered tights. Then, trying to get away from the well-wishers, her limp inevitably exaggerated by the knowledge of those watching eyes, the realization that they were waiting for her to tumble again, was an additional purgatory.

But no one was watching now. The deck was deserted and curtains had been drawn over the large recessed oblong windows of the public rooms facing on to the deck so that the gloomy weather might not affect the high spirits of the travellers inside. Outside, the bulkhead-type shutters which fitted into the recess, closing the windows off from high, stormy seas, were fastened back against the side, looking faintly decorative, but able to deliver a nasty bruise if one were to stumble against them. But she was not going to stumble.

She moved forward, despite the slipperiness of the deck, with a new confidence. She could be as slow or as awkward as she liked, there was no one to exclaim or gush out unwanted pity.

The full force of the wind hit her in a gust that sent her breath back into her throat as she left the shelter of the covered promenade deck. She could see whitecaps topping the waves that leapt like hungry flames from the deeper swell of the ocean a short distance ahead. Beyond that distance, a solid wall of mist cut off any view. They *were* heading into heavy weather.

The *Beatrice Cenci* shimmied uneasily as a wave slapped her broadside. Susan quickly rounded the open space of the bow to gain the shelter of the promenade again. A veil of dampness enveloped her, clinging wetly to her face and hair. Perhaps once round the deck would be enough. She did not feel like changing again, and she certainly didn't want to sit through the film in damp clothing.

Aft, just short of the open space of the stern, denuded now of deck-chairs, a heavy door led back into the warmth and comfort of the public rooms. She struggled briefly with the door, which seemed more than ordinarily reluctant to open and let the clammy chill of the encroaching storm inside.

The door capitulated suddenly, with a hiss of compressed air, and she stumbled into the warm, brightly lit passageway. She steadied herself against the inner wall momentarily and glanced at her watch. Three-quarters of an hour before the film was due to start; too early to go down to the cinema and she wasn't really in the mood to go back to her cabin. She snapped open her handbag, pulled out a Kleenex and dabbed thoughtfully at her face and hair and the moisture shining on her arms.

A metallic voice had begun calling the numbers for the Bingo enthusiasts in the card room opposite. Behind her, music was strumming softly in the "Night Club" and a muted shuffle kept time to the swish of metal brushes on the drum. They were dancing. She couldn't go in there.

She plunged into the lounge amidship, hurrying through it for the shelter of the quieter rooms at the front of the ship. Some of the faces that turned towards her as she moved through the lounge were beginning to be familiar now. She smiled at a professor who was one of her table-mates, but didn't pause. With his penchant for everything Italian, he would undoubtedly be going to the film, and she would rather sit by herself, so that she could duck out if she found it boring. She suspected that he would not admit it if he did find it boring, and that ducking out would be as frowned on as cutting a class.

As she approached the glass double doors at the end of the lounge, one of them swung open for her, held by a ship's officer with an inordinate amount of gold braid streeling casually around his sleeve.

"Signorina," he beamed. His attitude, his smile, his

eyes, all conveyed the impression that here was a shipboard romance, should she be so inclined. Automatic, of course. They all behaved this way to the female passengers.

"Thank you." She swept through the door without a backward glance. She heard the ghost of a regretful sigh, then the sound of the door swinging shut. She knew that he had continued on his way into the lounge.

The narrow Gothic arch that formed the portal to the Borgia Bar loomed just ahead on the left, and she shied away from it instinctively. In her opinion, they had overdone that particular bit of decor. Whether the designer had intended it to be amusing or picturesque, so far as she was concerned, he had failed. It seemed grim and sinister to her, with a brooding atmosphere the Borgias themselves would have felt all too much at home in.

Or perhaps it was simply that the Borgia Bar was not meant to appeal to women. Certainly, there never seemed to be any women patronizing it. And the male occupants, who had appeared perfectly friendly and welcoming outside, seemed to radiate a bleak hostility once settled within its dark fastnesses.

Opposite the bar, a less formidable arch led into the quiet harbour of the library. The rasp of a key turning in the lock of one of the glass-fronted bookcases drew her into the library. It must be open now, and it would be a good idea to get a book while there was still likely to be a good selection. Tomorrow, when the other passengers realized the weather, there would be a run on the library. One could laze with eyes closed in a deck-chair in good weather but, when it was too stormy to go outside and passengers were marooned in the public rooms, the frail bulwark of a book was one's only defence against boredom, and against the aggressive sociability of other passengers who would rove like marauders through the public rooms, seeking the prey of a captive audience.

Of the two large bookcases against the inner walls flanking the doorway, one held English language books, the other Italian. As befitted the new flagship of a proud fleet, the books were the latest, bright in their shining unrumpled jackets. Smaller unprotected bookshelves against the outer wall, beneath the portholes, held a smattering of paperbacks and books in other languages, some of which had obviously been left behind by departing passengers and annexed by the librarian to build up stock for the minority passengers, mostly French and German, it would appear from the books.

Behind the gleaming dark richness of the librarian's desk, the satin sheen of rich leather bindings enclosed two sets of encyclopaedias—one in English, one in Italian. Throughout the not-overlarge room, skilfully placed lamps turned chair-and-table combinations into private islands for study and reflection. Glossy magazines dotted the tables, their pools of colour an invitation to relax and browse.

Susan moved forward eagerly. The glass-fronted case of English books was open, the glass swinging out, then tapping back against its latch in rhythm with the sway of the ship. Careless of someone not to have closed it properly, but the librarian was not in sight.

She caught the glass door on the outward swing and held it open, studying the array of books. There was almost too good a choice. She saw several she had been intending to get, but the crowded events of the past few weeks had left her little time for reading. And the duration of the voyage would not give her time to read more than one or two. She must make a difficult choice.

As she pulled down half a dozen to carry over to one of the tables for a more leisurely selection, the glass door swung against her back with some force. She cried out, startled, and momentarily off-balance.

She caught the edge of a shelf, steadying herself, and was dismayed to find, when she turned, that someone had heard her cry. A darker shadow had arisen from the shadows of one of the chairs and was moving towards her.

"Are you all right?"

"Yes, of course." Then, aware that she should not brush him aside so ungraciously, she added. "The door swung and struck me, that was all. I wasn't expecting it—I was startled."

He remained standing. She could see now that she had not noticed him in the shadows because he was dressed in black. A starched white strip gleamed around his throat.

"Yes. The sea appears to be getting rougher."

She turned away, pointedly closing the glass door and making sure the latch was secure. When she turned back, he was still there, watching. She crossed to the nearest table and chair, aware that her limp was worse. Sheer nervousness always made it more pronounced when strange eyes were watching, when she most wanted to be able to walk normally.

Uncertainly, he re-seated himself after she had gained her own chair. Smiling apologetically, he returned to his book, but with an air that suggested he might be available for conversation were she so inclined.

She noticed, with some amusement, that he had chosen a science-fiction novel. A form of professional curiosity, she wondered? Taking a look at what the competition were serving up? Or did they think of it that way? Not that she had ever been particularly religious, but she had never noticed the clergy admitting to any other life than the one they were existing in and the one they preached. If other life-forms were eventually discovered in the process of space exploration, it would be interesting to see what the established clergy would come up with in the way of justification or explanation. Perhaps the good padre was already concerned about the problem and wanted to see what other minds hypothesized on the subject.

He glanced up from his book unexpectedly and caught her eyes on him. He smiled tentatively and she produced an equally tentative smile before disengaging glances and focusing firmly on her pile of books. She was not—she hoped she had signalled it forcibly enough—in a sociable mood. Unfortunately, it appeared that he was. She could feel his eyes on her as she picked up the top book and scanned the blurb.

The *Beatrice Cenci* tilted suddenly, toppling the pile of books. Two fell to the floor. He had picked them up before she could brace herself to lean over for them and replaced them on her table.

"It's only to be expected this time of year, I suppose," he offered. "Crossing this late, we run into the hurricane season."

"Hurricanes? This far out at sea?"

"Oh, perhaps not a hurricane itself." He spoke quickly, as though she needed reassurance. "But some of the weather associated with it . . . strong gales . . . high seas . . ." He trailed off uncertainly, looking at her face anxiously.

Perhaps it had been no more than an awkward conversational gambit. He had obviously been aching to talk to her ever since she had come into the room. Why not let him? She shrugged mentally. What could be more respectable than a priest?

"Surely," she said, "the ship would have posted some warnings if it were going to get really rough. The crew would—" She broke off.

One of the officers had just entered the library. He beamed at them and nodded casually. Then, still elaborately casual, he began moving around the room, stopping and stooping here and there.

After the first few times, the pattern began to emerge, they could discern what he was doing. He was stopping at the lighter chairs, strewn seemingly at random around the library, between the table-and-chair heavy islands. Yet not at random. Each chair was centred over a small recessed brass ring in the floor, hidden beneath a detachable flap of carpet. He fumbled beneath the seats of those chairs, pulling down a brass hook, then flipped back the small square of carpet and fitted the hook into the ring in the floor, and moved off—leaving the chairs securely anchored. They wouldn't slide across the room or tip over now, no matter how rough a sea tossed the ship about.

"There's no danger—" Meeting her eyes, the cleric spoke quickly again. "It's merely a precaution . . . most wise of them . . ."

How ironic, she thought, how very ironic. She had refused to fly in case . . . "PROVIDED ALWAYS . . ." And now
they were heading into hurricane seas. How very ironic if
Eric were to inherit the estate after all.

"No danger at all—" The good Father was still trying to
reassure her.

"I was going to the film." She selected two books and
moved to replace the others in the bookcase. "It's purported
to be a comedy. I suppose they'll still be showing it."

"Of course. Indeed, yes. A little thing like this is
nothing to worry about. Just a few hours, perhaps less. They
may change course and sail around it. Everything will certainly continue as usual."

"Yes, I suppose so." She snapped the bookcase shut
and glanced at her watch. Time to get down to the cinema
then, if she wanted a good seat.

"A comedy, eh?" He fell into step at her side. "That
sounds like an excellent idea. I could—I'm sure we both
could—use a good laugh."

Chapter 8

Some time during the night they had turned the foghorn on. It had brought Butler sitting bolt upright in his bed, his hand plunging beneath the pillow for the revolver he had not carried since he left the Syndicate, certainly should not have carried on this assignment, with Customs examination to face at the other end of the voyage. Strange, how the old reflexes lingered, long past any real need for them.

He took several deep breaths, orienting himself, then forced himself to recline again. They had slowed engines, too. The *Beatrice Cenci* was moving at a statelier pace—like a dowager queen rather than a racy young filly—picking her way meticulously through watery furrows, gaining in steadiness what she had lost in speed.

Carefully, with a discipline of long practice, Butler controlled his breathing, trying to think of pleasant things, even of triumphs as long distant as that revolver whose mirage still shimmered in his memory in moments of surprise or extreme stress.

Breathe in, breathe out. Breathe in, breathe out. That was it. That was better. It had always been the same. *Keep your cool, man.* That was the Gospel now, as then. *Breathe in, breathe out.*

Remember the time when St. Louis Moe got too big for his breeches? When he'd thought he could take over the whole Syndicate and get away with it? Remember that dark hotel room, with all the lights suddenly going on like a surprise birthday party? Remember the look on St. Louis Moe's face as the cement had gurgled around his feet?

Breathe in, breathe out.

Butler slept again, a smile on his face.

He woke again at the rustle at the door. Again bolt upright, again groping for the non-existent gun. This time, aware of a thin film of perspiration on his forehead.

That was bad. It was taking him longer to get oriented. Once, he would have known where he was, which assignment he was on, what the procedure was going to be, within a split-second of waking.

Something about this damned assignment was getting to him. What?

Deep and peremptory, the foghorn hooted overhead. *Make way for the Beatrice Cenci. The bella Beatrice.*

Maybe that was it. It was all taking too long. What kind of nuts wasted their time at sea, doing nothing, when a jet could lift them up and deposit them where they wanted to be within hours? This was the twentieth century—and they were still trying to live in the days of the China Clippers. They were all crazy—that was probably what was disturbing him about this assignment.

He withdrew his hand from under the pillow. If he didn't watch himself, he'd be going for the old shoulder holster next. Those days were over. As dead as the Dodo— as the China Clipper.

Leaning back, he fought for relaxation again, but it wouldn't come. There *had* been someone—something—at the door.

Moving stealthily, he stretched out a hand and abruptly switched on the light. There was no one in the doorway. Naturally not. He had expected, maybe, the Pope on a Wop ship like this?

Still frozen, only his eyes moving, he quartered the cabin. No one there.

The *Beatrice Cenci* shuddered, dipped, and shuddered again. The rough effect was that of performing a figure 8. Butler gave a faint shudder himself.

Then a blur of white at the foot of the door caught his eyes. He threw back the covers and advanced upon it cautiously. It was too flat and small to presage much danger. He stooped and picked it up, pulling it towards him to release the segment still underneath the door.

The ship's newspaper and the passenger list.

He carried them back to the bunk, pulling the sheet and blanket back over him to ward off the chill of the air-conditioning. This time he was able to relax, the point of possible danger pinpointed and nullified.

Yesterday, the ship's newspaper had been left in his cabin when the steward made up the bunk. Today, they were getting into the swing of things. It was the midpoint, the voyage half-way over. The ties with the shore loosened, the crew were functioning as a collective, self-determining unit. To put it more crudely, they were on the stick because they had their eyes on the tips coming up.

He glanced at the newspaper. Nothing that could really interest him in it—mostly just the bare bones of international situations which meant nothing to him and over which he had no control. A few titbits of gossip for those who couldn't feel comfortable without knowing who the President had honoured at a reception, or what show the latest Nine-Days'-Wonder had graced with the Presence last night. The rest was the purely parochial doings scheduled for the ship itself: "11:00 a.m.—Ship's Concert in the cocktail lounge (recorded), coffee will be served" . . . "2:30—Horse-racing in the main lounge" . . . "4:00—Repeat of last night's film in the cinema" . . . "8:00 p.m.—Sneak preview of new Hollywood film in the cinema" . . . "10:30—Dancing and Cabaret in the Night Club" . . . "Clocks will be turned ahead one hour tonight" . . . Ad. for the ship's shops and a few tourist traps in the port they were heading for.

Butler grunted and tossed the newspaper aside. He focused sharply on the passenger list. That, now, was more interesting.

He fingered the stiff white cardboard folder appreciatively. Nice, very nice, they did things up brown. The coloured and embossed miniature of the *Beatrice Cenci* on the outside was another damned work of art. Probably done by one of the lazy bums whose work was on exhibit in those flouncy shops downstairs.

He opened the folder and flipped over the pages, his eyes skimming the neatly-printed columns of names, all in strictly alphabetical order, all with their allotted cabin number, so that passengers who wished to contact new friends did not have to waste the time of the ship's switchboard operator with endless enquiries.

Funny, how fast you got to recognize people, how many names were already familiar, fitting themselves to faces without any conscious mental effort.

He checked the name he sought. Yes, still the same cabin number. Hadn't moved, after all—but it had been worth waiting, to make sure.

Besides, it was the mark of an amateur to make your hit too early. The professional knew you needed time to look around, to spy out the possible avenues of escape—not that there could be many on board a ship. And that was another reason why too early a move would have been dangerous— it would have left everyone on board with too much time to conduct an investigation. Days in which to ask questions, check alibis, look for the slip that might have been made due to unfamiliarity with shipboard routine.

But today was the half-way mark in the voyage. Tomorrow would bring the last night out, with all its attendant excitements. Passengers would be packing, putting their luggage out ready to be taken ashore, planning what to wear for the Gala Dinner. They would all be preoccupied with their own concerns, too busy to pay much attention to what was happening around them. Anything untoward would either not be noticed or later related in so garbled a version that little useful could be construed from it.

And the *Beatrice Cenci* had a schedule to keep to. The ship was due for a quick turnaround at Genoa and the return voyage to New York. She could not spare too much time to stop and search for a missing passenger; neither could her departing passengers be delayed for too long in Genoa. And, once ashore, their memories would begin to blur, the days aboard ship to seem like shadows from another life.

Everything would be brushed aside as just one of the unfortunate accidents that sometimes happen on a ship. The opening anecdote of their stories about their trip to Europe—those who knew what had happened. There would be many, of course, who would have no idea that anything had happened at all. It wasn't the sort of thing the shipping line would want publicized. In fact, they'd try to hush it up as much as possible. Working for themselves, they'd be working for him, too. That was the way to arrange things. Nobody wants to know too much, so nobody looks too closely at the details, so everybody is happy.

Butler looked at his watch: 6:00 a.m. Too early to get up. Besides, he was feeling pleasantly drowsy now. The foghorn still sounded at rhythmic intervals—keeping danger at bay. Now that he was used to it, he almost liked it.

Butler turned off the light and slithered back into a recumbent position. The ship had settled down to a pleasant rocking motion, reminiscent of the hammocks of his brief childhood. Soothing, especially the knowledge that no wise guy was going to come up behind and tip him out of *this* hammock, this cosy little niche. For a long time now, he had been the only one doing the tipping.

Butler relaxed, feeling sleep rising like a gentle tide to engulf him. So far, so good. No problems. The initial contact had been made. She could have no suspicion, no idea that she was even in danger. Everything was smooth and easy. It was going to be another effortless, flawless job. With the extra bonus of a European trip thrown in. He might even stay over there for a while, take a look at some of those places people were always talking about. Sample the booze and broads in a few different countries—there would be money enough. He could have a good time before coming back and picking up his next assignment. He might even be able to pick up a couple of contracts over there. Who knew? It might even be a good place to stay for a couple of years, if the going was good.

After all, lots of people went there to retire. Not that he was contemplating that. Retirement had never figured in any of his dreams. He had always enjoyed his work too much.

Chapter 9

"I don't like it," Mrs. Abercrombie said. Her hands made that futile, brushing-aside gesture again before she seemed to notice them and clasped them tightly in her lap.

"It's all right," Val soothed. "It will only be for a minute." She kept her voice professionally cool, allowing no hint of the sympathy she felt to creep in. She was not altogether happy about using the lift herself. There was something claustrophobic about an elevator in a ship—more so than in ordinary life. Yet they had to use it. She could not take the wheelchair up the stairs, nor could she allow Mrs. Abercrombie to climb stairs—especially not in weather like this.

Val braced the wheelchair against the roll of the ship as they both watched the red indicator light slide to their level.

"Utter nonsense?" Mrs. Abercrombie said. "I am perfectly capable of taking a turn around the deck without the aid of this—this *contraption*!" She slapped a rim of rubber contemptuously. "I can manage quite well simply holding on to your arm."

The *Beatrice Cenci* gave a shudder nearly as violent as Val's at that idea. Of course, it was a good sign when the patient began getting fractious, but she could have wished for Mrs. Abercrombie's improvement to hold off until a more opportune moment. Until they reached shore, say. It was going to be difficult enough to manoeuvre a safely-seated Mrs. Abercrombie in a wheelchair today—at least the chair would provide some protection, insulation. The thought of trying to keep an ambulatory Mrs. Abercrombie from falling was enough to provide the stuff of nightmares for years to come. And she already had enough nightmare-fodder to last the rest of her life.

A bell sounded and, with a brisk snick, the lift doors parted to reveal an occupant on the verge of stepping out, who retreated as he saw them. He glanced up at the indicator to verify the level he was at and shook his head.

"So you're the ones who've hijacked me," he greeted. "Here—" he stepped forward to catch the footrest of Mrs. Abercrombie's wheelchair— "let me help you with that."

Mrs. Abercrombie's legs gave a minuscule twitch—as though she contemplated kicking him in his foolish amiable face.

"That isn't necessary, thank you." Val was scarcely less annoyed herself, as he tilted the wheelchair at an awkward angle, threatening to spill Mrs. Abercrombie on to the floor.

"No trouble at all." He dropped the footrest with a bone-jarring thump. Mrs. Abercrombie made a faint inarticulate sound which was as much a snarl as a moan.

"Aren't you going to introduce us?" he demanded of Val.

"I'm afraid I don't know your name," Val disclaimed hastily. Heaven forbid that Mrs. Abercrombie should think she was friendly with this boor.

"Easily fixed—" He held out his hand. "I'm Dick Slade—Dick to my friends. Slade's Manufacturing—perhaps you've heard of—"

"I'm afraid not." Mrs. Abercrombie closed her eyes, pointedly ignoring the outstretched hand.

"No," Val seconded, keeping too occupied with minor adjustment to the wheelchair to have a hand free.

"Oh, well. I guess you wouldn't anyway—" He let his hand fall to his side. "It's pretty specialized manufacturing—mechanical toys, components, that sort of thing."

The doors slid closed and the elevator moved upwards. Just then the *Beatrice Cenci* gave a dip and a roll.

"I don't like it!" The words seemed jerked out of Mrs. Abercrombie against her will. Her voice was tight with the effort at control. "I don't like it at all!"

"I know just what you mean, lady." Dick Slade nodded

his head sagely. "And I don't blame you one bit. Especially—" He broke off, as though aware of an impending indiscretion.

"Especially—*what*?" Mrs. Abercrombie's eyes opened to glare at him suspiciously.

"Well . . . here—and now . . ." His shoulder writhed uneasily and decided on a shrug. "*You* know."

"Know—*what*?" Mrs. Abercrombie was not going to let him get away with innuendoes.

"Shut up here in this little box—" He began clarifying, oblivious to Val's gestures to keep quiet and change the subject. "Suppose we should get stuck—elevators do, you know. I should think this elevator jamming would be just about the first thing that would happen in an emergency. And we wouldn't even know if the ship was sinking—until it was too late and the water began coming in under the door."

"I see." Mrs. Abercrombie had begun to get a faint rim of perspiration over her top lip.

"Nothing like that could possibly happen," Val said firmly. "Ships don't sink in this day and age—not passenger liners like this."

"No?" Something ancient and jaundiced peeped at her out of his eyes. "What about the *Andrea Doria*?"

"Oh, but—"

"That had radar and all the latest equipment. And that—" he reminded her with gloomy relish— "that was an Italian ship, too."

Mrs. Abercrombie's hands had begun to tremble; she clenched them tightly in her lap and stared straight ahead at the elevator doors.

Wasn't this an extraordinarily slow elevator? Something of her fear began to communicate itself to Val. Shouldn't they have reached the promenade deck by this time?

The *Beatrice Cenci* lurched in a sidestep, just as the elevator shuddered to a halt. The door parted about three inches, shivered indecisively, and snapped shut again like the jaws of a steel trap.

Mrs. Abercrombie's hands twisted convulsively just

once, then fought themselves to stillness once more. Her breathing had become audible.

"It's just a temporary fault," Val assured her quickly. "The crew will—"

"The crew will be the first ones into the lifeboats at any sign of trouble," Dick Slade said with confidence. "They always are. I remember the reports—"

"The first reports always say things like that," Val said coldly. She was beginning to hate the man. How could he be so stupid? Couldn't he see how upset Mrs. Abercrombie was getting? It wasn't enough that he reminded her of all the smug, self-satisfied, petty-minded persecutors she had so lately known, he had to be an actively malicious mischief-maker, as well.

"And," she pointed out, "it always turns out to have been the kitchen hands. The crew were completely honourable and reported to their stations."

"Oh, sure, sure," he placated. "Don't get huffy. I was just—"

The doors opened again, this time sliding all the way back and remaining open.

Outside, a glowering ship's officer sketched a salute and moved to help with the wheelchair. Had he been able to hear what was being said inside the lift? Had he registered the slurs on his ship and his nationality?

From the murderous glare he shot at Dick Slade, it seemed highly probable. The next time they were in the Borgia Bar together, Mr. Slade might do well to watch his drink carefully. Old customs could linger on—especially when the provocation was severe.

At least he was gentler—or more experienced in these matters—than Dick Slade. He moved smoothly and gracefully as a cat; the wheelchair flowed out on to the promenade level.

"Signora." He straightened up, looked at them both searchingly. "Signorina, I am Angelo. If you have any trouble at any time. If anything happen. You find me. You come straight to me. I will take care of you."

* * *

Guido was fretful as Gloria laced him into his little harness. He was bored with it and incubating mutiny, but she was not going to take him outside the cabin without it—no matter how much he fussed. The ship was rolling too heavily in the deep swells of rough water, while the foghorn sounded a grim reminder of the weather waiting for those who ventured on deck.

Guido must have some fresh air, but he must also be kept under control. A wet deck, a thick fog, one steep roll of the ship—and that tiny beloved body could slide across the deck and under the guard rails to disappear into the deep. No question of stopping the ship in time, or of being able to locate him, even if he could keep afloat in the midst of those monster waves.

"There!" She secured the final buckle to the leading reins and stood up, looking down at him. So tiny—and providing so many complications, so much to think about and consider. Her hostage to fortune—one of them.

Life had been so much simpler on other voyages. Yet would she wish those carefree days back again? Give up all she had gained—even if there were moments when she counted up the cost?

No. She stooped and gathered Guido into her arms but, as she began to lift him, the ship suddenly lurched sideways and she was flung heavily down on one knee.

That did it. She abandoned any idea of carrying Guido. It was obviously going to be difficult enough to keep her own balance, without endangering Guido. Better let him trot around on his own two little feet—he wouldn't have so far to fall.

"Come on, honey." She tugged at the reins hopefully while Guido stood firm. "Giddyap," she coaxed.

Guido considered the idea, with Lorenzo's own mulish expression on his face.

"Giddyap!" Smiling, Gloria jiggled the reins hopefully again.

"Yap!" His face cleared, he gave a little bound and started for the door at a prance, straining against the leash. Crisis over, all sunshine and sweetness now.

Just like his father; Gloria opened the door with a faint sigh. She was really going to have her hands full in a few more years. Both of them—and the business, too.

At least, Lorenzo seemed to be settling down now. Since Guido's arrival, he had begun to change. Slower to anger—although, heaven knew, anyone without prior experience of it would still call his a hair-trigger temper—and more given to deep brooding silences, from which he emerged in a curious mood.

He had also been taking a great deal more interest in the shop. She frowned, not entirely sure that that was a development she liked. He upset the staff, demanding a perfection which was unachievable in view of the circumstances. He always got most insistent in his demands during a period of panic, when everyone had enough to do trying to sort out the existing crisis without coping with his improbable requests. Also, they were unaccustomed to the peremptory giving of orders.

In time, no doubt it *would* be a good thing to set up another store—that projected branch in a resort—for Lorenzo to manage. With a staff he had hired and trained himself, unable to make comparisons with a more easygoing boss, he would undoubtedly find his feet. But he was so impatient. It was so hard to make him understand that these things took time, that it was better to wait another couple of years to consolidate fully the gains being made in the original shop. If he had his way, he would have had them borrow from the bank and set up a chain of shops—and all in the name of an "empire" for Guido to inherit some day. At the rate Lorenzo wanted to progress, all Guido would inherit would be a pile of newspaper clippings about his parents' bankruptcy hearing and a load of debts it would take forty years to pay off.

She had intended to take Guido up on deck, but her thoughts automatically strayed towards the Galleries. She was making progress there—becoming friendly with the girls in the shops. She hadn't mentioned her idea to any of them yet, but before the voyage was over she would. For today, however, it would be enough to work a bit more at cementing the friendly relationships. She also wanted to find out the name of the manufacturer and supplier of a certain—

The *Beatrice Cenci* heaved her bow into the air, seemed to hesitate, and then slammed down into the swell of an oncoming wave. The effect was like that of a missed step.

Guido sat down abruptly with a surprised expression. It had been a long time since his legs had been so unreliable. He looked up at her with protest.

"All right, baby." She had been flung against the wall of the companionway herself, but recovered quickly.

"Nothing to worry about." She stooped and set him on his feet again. "It's just the way funny old ships behave. We're not on land, you know." She smiled.

"Oh no." He had raised his arms to be lifted and carried, but she shook her head. "No, that's not a good idea in this weather. We'll both walk—that will be safer."

The elevator would be safer than the stairs, too. One of those rock-and-roll antics the ship had been indulging in during the night could send Guido toppling down the stairs, collecting a fine assortment of bruises, maybe even a couple of broken bones.

And wouldn't that be great? To bring his precious son back to Lorenzo all done up in plaster-casts. The faintest scratch or bruise brought wild recriminations from Lorenzo—a woman's place was in the home—if she had been taking care of Guido properly such a thing could not have happened. Just wait until some of the inevitable childhood illnesses began to strike: measles, chicken-pox, mumps, scarlet fever. It didn't bear thinking about.

They had just missed the elevator. She saw the starched white uniform disappear into it and knew that there wouldn't have been room for them anyway—that wheelchair would take up a lot of space.

Still, that was an idea—the nurse, not the wheelchair. Perhaps she could hire a nurse—more for Lorenzo than Guido—when the kiddy ills started. With tranquillizers and constant medical attention, they might pull Lorenzo through safely. Guido, of course, would make his own way with flying colours, like all kids.

Lorenzo. She frowned, bracing herself automatically against a newly-developed hopscotching motion of the ship. Absorbed in her thoughts, it seemed but a moment until the elevator slid to their level again and the doors swooped open to receive them.

Lorenzo. At the back of her mind, there arose again the last brief disturbing glimpse she had had of him. Standing close to Joe, heads together, turning to watch the ship pull away from the shore. There had been something conspiratorial, almost furtive, about them. As though they were hatching out some plan they knew she would disapprove of.

But what? She knew instinctively that she would disapprove of practically anything Joe thought up. He hated her. He spent a great deal of time egging Lorenzo on to actions that would annoy her. If he could, he would take advantage of every moment she was away to manoeuvre Lorenzo on to ever more dangerous pathways.

Why? Did he still hope he could break up the marriage? And, even if he did, what good would it do him? She had Guido now—a child of her own. Anything there might eventually be to inherit would go to Guido. It was just too bad that Joe and—yes, probably Pauline, too—had written her off as not the marrying kind. Joe had spent too many years shrugging off his own failures and inadequacies with the thought, "Never mind, the kids will inherit their Aunt Gloria's money and we'll all be sitting pretty yet."

They'd never mentioned it, but she'd known that idea was always at the back of Joe's mind. Perhaps it was the cause of so much of the antipathy between them. How dare he assume that she was going to die first. She was younger than he was. She went around a lot more, of course, and there was always more chance that she might die in a plane crash or in an automobile accident on one of her buying trips than that Joe might expire during the usual high point of his evening, which was sitting in front of the television set with a glass of beer.

How Pauline stood it, she'd never know. Once, not

more than half joking, she'd offered Pauline the money to finance a divorce. What was the good of being a successful business-woman if you couldn't provide your loved ones with the little luxuries of life? Except that, with a slob like Joe, divorce wasn't a luxury, but a necessity. Surprisingly, Pauline had not taken advantage of the offer. In fact, she had probably told Joe about it.

They had never been on particularly cordial terms, and relations between them had worsened from that point onwards. Joe's resentment had been mostly a silent, smouldering one—breaking out only in snide remarks masquerading as "jokes" or "kidding." Until her marriage.

With the advent of Lorenzo, Joe had found a newer, subtler way of striking at her. Lorenzo, who was still too unsure of his position, of his grasp of the English language, of her, to be able to grapple with the innuendoes slyly and consistently slipped into every conversation by Joe.

It was not that Lorenzo liked Joe, or even trusted him particularly. It was that Lorenzo, from a completely male-oriented society, accustomed to women keeping in their place—which was the home and the Church—was bewildered and resentful in this new world where women could hold the power, dominate businesses, make vital decisions, without suitable and prolonged consultation with their lord and master.

And Joe played upon this disgruntled bewilderment, insinuating that Lorenzo wasn't a proper man if he couldn't keep his wife under control—if she went on doing everything without consulting him. Sure, she'd done it before—but what did that matter? Now she had a man to look up to, and she ought to be looking up to him.

Joe had tried less subtle methods—but only once. She had taken care of that.

"Gee, I'm sorry," she had said, when Pauline came to her shortly afterwards to "borrow" the school fees for the kids. "But I'm broke—totally. I've had so many extra expenses lately—" Holding Pauline's eyes, she had listed them: "The new car, two new suits, an evening gown, a cocktail dress, extra hairdos, that full-day session at Elizabeth Arden's—and there'll probably be more extra expenses next month . . . After all—" she had smiled at Pauline, not bothering to keep the steel out of her voice— "if *your* husband is going to go around introducing *my* husband to younger and prettier women, then I'm going to have to spend all my spare cash on myself to beat the competition."

So, it was no more subtle than Joe had been, but Pauline had received the message loud and clear. And the icy black glitter in Joe's eyes confirmed that she had relayed it to him, probably with embellishments—which wouldn't do him any harm. He had never tried that trick again, even though he had found others.

But the gloves were off after that, and his eyes had never again been able to conceal their "drop dead" glitter when he looked at her. If he had been a stronger character, she might have been afraid of him. As it was, she shrugged mentally, he was a petty, malicious troublemaker, but hadn't the nerve to take any more positive steps. Just a small-timer, making waves around the edges, that was Joe.

And, as Lorenzo grew more sure of himself in the American business world, began making his own friends and contacts, Joe's influence would wane. It would take time, that was all.

The elevator stopped with a little bounce and the doors slithered open in reluctant slow motion. She urged Guido forward before the machinery could change its mind and snap the doors shut again, which seemed probable right now.

The *Beatrice Cenci* shuddered, momentarily her lights seemed to dim.

Guido halted warily, bracing himself against whatever new trick was going to be played upon him by the strange floor which looked so solid and familiar, but possessed a life and a will of its own. He turned and looked back at her uneasily, as though already recognizing that she was a broken reed in a situation like this.

Then his gaze shifted beyond her and brightened. He lifted his arms. "Da-da," he said, quite plainly. "Da-da."

Gloria whirled about, eyes shining, heart beating ridiculously.

The lights flickered fitfully, then regained their former brilliance. The dim figure at the far end of the corridor stood out clearly, the light glinting off gilt buttons, off rows of gold braid on his cuffs.

It was nothing, of course. Could have been nothing except that Guido had reached the stage of connecting the word Da-da with a man—any man. And thank God Lorenzo wasn't here to have one of his fits of hysterical frenzy over the thought of *his* son thinking any other man was his daddy. In most families, such childish mistakes could be laughed off. Lorenzo would have demanded a full explanation—perhaps even a blood test. Lorenzo had no sense of humour where his bloodline was concerned—or his precious honour.

"Da-da," Guido said firmly. He stumbled forward, arms still outstretched, lurching towards the advancing figure. She had dropped his reins in her disappointment and he was taking full advantage of his brief freedom.

"Hah!—Bambino!" The officer, the one they called Angelo, stooped and picked up Guido, tossing him ceilingwards, catching him again, sure-footed as a mountain goat while the ship skipped from mountainous wavetop to mountainous wavetop.

Guido crowed with delight, boneless baby fingers raking in his descent at Angelo's face, at his shoulders, at his jacket.

Angelo frowned abruptly and swung Guido away from him, holding him at arm's length. "Basta, now," he said. "Enough. You get too excited. Is not good." He set Guido on the floor and met Gloria's eyes over the child's head. His own eyes had darkened.

"I show . . ." His hand—the one not steadying Guido—darted for his inside jacket pocket, hesitated and plunged. He withdrew it with a plastic folder of photographs which he extended to Gloria. "*My* bambini," he said proudly.

"How nice." She knew when she was licked. Forcing a smile, she tried to sound enthusiastic. "They're darling!"

It was the usual assortment of smug, overdressed brats. Although the boys outweighed the girls in numbers, the sheer awfulness of flounced dresses, tiny gold sleepers glittering in pierced ears and the knowing smirks made the girls appear worse horrors. In actuality, there was probably nothing to choose between them. Gloria gave a shudder for what she had been spared. Had Guido turned out to be a Gilda, Lorenzo would undoubtedly have insisted on the pink ruffles, the pierced ears, the whole terrifying lot.

"Maria, Umberto, Lola . . ." Why did people always think you cared who was who? Gloria felt her smile grow strained as the itemized catalogue continued.

Guido snatched suddenly at the tempting shiny plastic accordion folder and nearly succeeded in capturing it. Gloria caught his hand and pulled him back just in time.

"I'm afraid he's restless," she apologized. "We ought to be getting along. I've promised him some candy and—"

A ship's bell sounded a peremptory summons. The ship's officer snapped the folder back into its case, glanced at his watch and shrugged. "*Scusi, Signora . . .*"

Something in the set of his shoulders as he strode away made Gloria check her own watch uneasily. It *was* an odd time for the ship's bell to sound—assuming it only sounded to signal the time. Of course, that was the only time she paid any attention to it, mentally translating the number of bells into the correct hour of the day. For all she knew, it was sounding continual signals to the crew about one thing or another, but she just hadn't registered the fact.

She shrugged her own shoulders. At the end of the passageway, the lights of the Gift Galleries glowed a welcoming beacon. Guido was watching her expectantly, already half-turned towards the promise of the shops, of candy, of admiration and spoiling from the salesgirls. He was getting a taste for the whole thing young—he'd be doing buying trips of his own in no time.

Maybe it wouldn't be a bad idea now to let him act as a test market for children's toys. A small range could easily be added to the boutique lines. Small, exclusive, imported toys—they ought to go down well.

"All right," she said, giving the reins a gentle tug. "Off we go. Off to the races."

The deck was wet and slippery with the mysterious oiliness that sea spray seemed to call up out of the deckboards. A white woolly cloud seemed to have wrapped itself tenaciously around the *Beatrice Cenci*, accompanying her rather than offering any hope that she might sail out on the other side. Her foghorn blared monotonously and hopelessly into it as though recognizing the futility of its lone voice making any difference in that thick blinding mist.

Ships no longer depended exclusively on their foghorns, Susan reminded herself firmly. They were equipped with radar these days, that narrow grey semicircle revolving endlessly at the top of the mast rising above the smokestacks. Like the foghorn, the smokestacks were no longer strictly necessary, merely a faintly reassuring reminder of the days when ships had been the monarchs of travel, their proud boast of the time they took measured in days rather than the hours of the upstart usurpers sweeping across the alien sky.

But there was nothing like having a solid deck under your feet—however much it tilted—nor the deep comforting swell of the Atlantic surging beneath the solid hull of a ship.

The *Beatrice Cenci* shimmied and seemed to try to sidestep a wave. Ahead of her, Susan saw the only other passenger who had had the courage to come on deck stagger and regain his footing. A steward had tried—with excessive delicacy—to warn her off coming on deck this afternoon, not realizing these conditions were to her liking. In weather like this, she was as sure-footed as anyone. The uncertain deck equalized all passengers, the ones with two good legs no longer had an advantage. The advantage lay with those who could adjust their balance to sudden changes in their gait—and she had had plenty of practice at that.

Ahead the figure turned, walked across the bleak deserted end of the sun deck, past the covered swimming pool, and turned again to continue his solitary promenade up the starboard side. She saw him stagger as the full force of the gale hit him, then slowly fight his way forward. He wasn't going to give up—and neither was she.

She pulled her coat tighter against the wet chill and ducked her head as she crossed the wide windswept stern herself. Beneath her feet, the white-painted shuffleboard lines gleamed with ghostly phosphorescence under their veiling mist. There wouldn't be many outdoor games played on this voyage.

Inside, the lights of the public rooms beckoned warmly. They were beginning to serve tea in the lounge. White-coated waiters could be seen moving among the tables, setting out cups and saucers beside waiting passengers. The ship's orchestra would have begun playing its usual teatime medley of soothing old favourites, but no thread of melody escaped to make itself heard above the wind.

It would be pleasant to turn her back on the icy afternoon, go inside and settle down to her book and a cup of hot tea with the delicate triangles of thin savoury sandwiches and tiny fancy cakes. But that would be too much like refusing a challenge—and she had never been able to do that.

She swung out in a wide curve before turning to head into the wind. Even then it stopped her dead for a moment, meeting her like a live force field, holding her suspended as she struggled to move. Force 9? Force 10? Higher? She had experienced nothing like it before.

It was almost a battle of wills: her own stubbornness against the blind inanimate rage of the storm. The fight to move her legs was as hard as those first steps had been so many years ago when she was relearning to walk after the accident.

She seemed to advance in slow-motion, the wind fighting to drive her backwards. Her breath was hurled back into her throat, tiny pinpoints of rain slashed at her unprotected face like needles.

The *Beatrice Cenci* juddered from stem to stern as she ploughed into heavier seas. The storm seemed to be increasing. If she were sensible, she ought to go inside now, have that hot comforting cup of tea and stop fighting the elements.

She slipped and nearly fell, but the pause while she caught her balance halted her progress and it was a fight to drive herself forward again. She exerted all her energy to move her leg forward, but the wind fought her to a standstill and again held her suspended like a puppet.

A faint panic seized her. If she couldn't move forward, she would be driven back, perhaps swept over the side. Without any witness to report the accident, to have the ship stopped, a lifeboat lowered, a search begun—provided always, there was any use at all in attempting a search in weather like this. *Provided always* . . .

And Eric would inherit, after all. The stud farm, the estate, the shareholdings—everything would go to him. He would win, after all—after all these years.

Half-sobbing, she felt the flood of adrenalin bring renewed energy to meet the challenge. Eric would *not* inherit. It was hers—it was all hers—and it had always been. Slowly, she began to move forward again, more warily now, edging away from the railing which now looked so powerless to be any protection to a body hurled against it by this gale. Hitting the rail broadside, it might be possible to cling to it. But, hurled off one's feet, a body would slide helplessly beneath the lower rail and disappear into the raging sea.

It was not going to happen to her! She had established a slow, even rhythm now, carrying her closer to the safety of the door at the end of the deck which would open into the warmth and companionship of the public rooms.

She was even beginning to enjoy the battle again, knowing that she was still able to rise to a challenge—as she always had been.

"*You can't make that fence! You'll never make that fence!*"

"*Yes, I can!*"

"No, you can't. You'd need a better horse than you've got. Thunderbolt isn't good enough!"

"Thunderbolt is the best horse in the world. Thunderbolt can take any fence!"

"Not that one! Don't you dare try it. You don't dare—"

"Yes, I do. I dare anything!"

Then the brief glorious moment of soaring . . . the terrible descent, pinned between Thunderbolt and the fence. The agony of pain and the worse agony of hearing Thunderbolt's anguished whinnies and knowing that she had betrayed him. She should never have forced him to that jump—it *was* too high—and Thunderbolt wasn't seasoned enough—either to take it or to refuse it, knowing it was beyond his powers. He had trusted her judgement and her faith in him. She had failed him—she had failed them both. She should have known better.

She should have known . . . Later, lying in the hospital bed, wondering if she would ever stop reliving those moments, stop hearing Thunderbolt's cries, the shot, and the abrupt ghastly silence, she knew that she had been a fool. Eric had deliberately played upon her daring and her pride, goading her as expertly as she had often watched him goading his school friends, bullying them with a relentless charm which did not count as bullying because it was mental pressure he was exerting rather than physical. But the effect was the same: Eric got what he wanted . . .

But not that time. And not now. Not ever again—

A hand shot out, seized her by the arm and pulled her into the lee of a pair of funnels.

"Whatever we're trying to prove," he said, "I think we've proved it well enough by now."

Professor Cook might be one of her tablemates, but that was no reason for his treating her like a recalcitrant pupil. She shook herself free of his grip, but could not quite bring herself to leave the shelter of the warm funnels and return to the open deck.

"They're serving tea," he said. "We might as well go inside and have some—after all, we're paying for it."

"I don't want any," she said. One of the funnels must

be leading up from the galley, it was blowing out a stream of warm air heavy with food odours and the smell of too much garlic. She began to feel faintly queasy.

"You'd better have some just the same," he said. His nose wrinkled. "I can't help feeling that tonight's menu is going to be a big mistake. But it's fatal to go without eating."

"They make these menus out weeks in advance." She felt obscurely driven to defend the kitchen staff. "They can't know they're going to run into weather like this."

"They know it's probable at this time of the year," he said. "Even so, they ought to be sufficiently flexible to re-arrange their menus or make substitutions when they run into heavy seas. They can't *want* a shipload of seasick passengers on their hands."

The *Beatrice Cenci* dipped and shuddered in a curious sideways motion which ensured that they simultaneously received a dash of icy sea spume in their faces along with a gust of garlic.

"What," Susan enquired ironically, "would you recommend for dinner on a night like this?"

"Hardtack, perhaps." He grinned suddenly and his whole face lightened and changed. "There were good reasons why the old ways were best."

"Not all of them," she said. "I'm sure there were cultures which would have taken one look at this sea and decided that Neptune was angry and could only be propitiated by a human sacrifice."

"Perhaps they were right." His face shuttered, the brooding darkness came back. "For all our science, we're a long way from knowing everything. It could take a couple more centuries before we really find out what's down there."

She shuddered, caught in a sudden chill which had nothing to do with the storm. She wished that she had not strayed off the safe conversational path into this dark byway.

"You're cold," he said. "Inside." He took her arm, urging her forward, buttressing her with his own strength. "We'll both feel less argumentative after tea."

After the moments in shelter, it was colder than ever in the open, but it was a relief to escape the garlic fumes. Susan noticed that the man adjusted his steps to her slower pace without comment and without apology. In any case, the brutal assault of the wind left them without breath to speak. In silence, they fought their way forward to the companionway door.

"Here we are," he wrestled the door open against the wind. "You know, people who walk the deck a lot—particularly in weather like this—are popularly supposed to be working out problems, or else having a shipboard romance. We ought to start some interesting rumours."

Chapter 10

At dinner, the waiters tried briefly to maintain order, then abandoned the unequal struggle. Passengers, already demoralized by the storm, halted uncertainly in the doorway, further disoriented by the vista of empty tables stretching out before them. Unable to recognize their own immediately, without any of the familiar faces landmarking it, they looked around for someone they did know and moved to that table.

After a few half-hearted attempts to shepherd their passengers to the right table, the waiters shrugged and allowed them to have their own way. One night ought not to make any difference when tipping time came. Besides, it was too easy for someone sitting alone at a table to begin feeling sorry for himself and start imagining the onset of seasickness. When there were others at the table, a certain pride kept one seated and trying to eat. Everyone knew that food was a powerful weapon against seasickness—in the preventive sense. A passenger who neglected the main course in favour of tea and toast was a passenger half-way to sick bay. It was a good night to be a waiter rather than a cabin steward.

"Fish!" Mrs. Abercrombie said decisively. "A dinner portion of fish—and no sauce of any kind." She looked around her table authoritatively.

"I have a theory," she announced, "that the best thing to eat in an ocean like this is something that already has an affinity with the ocean. After all, fish never get seasick, do they?"

"Fish," Valerie agreed, as the waiter's enquiring eye moved to her. It was as good a theory as any. It might even work.

The waiter made a notation on his pad and moved along.

"That sounds fine to me." They could have done without the company of the loud-mouthed Mr. Slade, but he had asked to join them when he found his own table deserted, and it would have been churlish to refuse. "Mrs. Abercrombie strikes me as a lady who knows what she's talking about. I'll go along with her judgement."

"Fish . . . Yes, I guess . . . the fish . . ." One by one, the others at the table endorsed Mrs. Abercrombie's decision.

"All fish," the waiter sighed. At least, it was going to make his work easier. "And vegetable? You like cheeps? The french fries?"

"Not french fries," Mrs. Abercrombie said firmly. She was blossoming as doyen of the gathering, happily aware that her age and experience were being looked to for guidance by the uninitiated.

"Plain boiled potatoes," she allowed them. "Or possibly mashed. But not the french fried. I have reason to believe," she explained, "that they are putting garlic into the frying oil. Which is all very well, in the ordinary way—but not on a night like tonight."

The waiter shrugged and rolled his eyes expressively, disclaiming all responsibility for the vagaries of the kitchen staff.

"'Heaven help a sailor on a night like this,' eh, Mrs. Abercrombie?" Dick Slade murmured with arch ribaldry.

"Heaven help all of us," Gloria grumbled. (Guido was in the cabin, nearly asleep when she left him, guarded by a stewardess who might have to leave at intervals to succour those more in need of her attention.) "I thought you sort of sailed through a storm—in one side and out the other. What's the matter with this one? It's been following us all the way like a mongrel stray."

The waiter shrugged again, likewise disclaiming responsibility for the vagaries of the weather. "Little tomato?" he coaxed. "Peas? Aubergine?"

"Nothing else for me, thank you," Mrs. Abercrombie

said. "Although," she conceded graciously to the others, "the peas *ought* to be harmless. I wouldn't advise tomatoes—especially with all the herbs they consider necessary to them."

Everyone refused the offered vegetables—even the peas. There was no point in taking chances. The waiter shrugged again and moved galleywards.

They sat in silence, except for the jingle of the cutlery as it clustered together then shivered apart with every vibration of the ship. The dining salon seemed twice its usual size with only occasional tables sparsely dotted with occupants.

The waiters huddled together at the far end, away from the galley doors through which they made infrequent and reluctant forays as though they, too, were not over-anxious to breathe too deeply of the highly spiced aromas of the cooking area.

"Here come the lovebirds," Dick Slade said. He gestured, directing their attention to the main entrance. The lame girl and the professor were poised in the doorway, surveying the room uncertainly.

"How do you know?" Gloria challenged.

"Easy, they were out together on deck all afternoon. In this weather. That's *got* to mean something. Haven't you heard—?" Although he was nominally answering Gloria, his eyes sought Mrs. Abercrombie's with a ghost of a twinkle, a proprietorial air. "Shipboard is a great place for romance to blossom?"

Mrs. Abercrombie bridled faintly. As though responding to an unspoken suggestion, she raised her hand to the couple. "Over here," she called. They moved automatically towards the group. Although there was no room at that table, they took the one next to it, making a cluster of survivors in that corner of the dining salon.

Well, why not? Valerie decided, after the first flush of surprise had faded. Mrs. Abercrombie was still what was known as "a fine figure of a woman." She was a widow, and Dick Slade had confided that he had recently buried his wife. Why shouldn't they get together?

It was her own opinion that Dick Slade was a crashing bore—but Mrs. Abercrombie had previously been married to a manufacturer, perhaps she didn't find them boring. She probably understood things like production schedules, forward planning, staff problems, delivery dates, and all the technicalities of a manufacturer's life. It could be an ideal match.

Of course, Mildred and Augustus might not think so. They had spent a lot of time dancing attendance on their step-aunt and it might not be entirely unjust to suspect that quite a lot of it was due to trying to ensure that there were no inheritance problems, rather than sheer affection. On the other hand, Dick Slade's economic status was still an unknown quantity. It was entirely possible that an alliance with him might double or treble their eventual inheritance rather than deplete it.

In any case, she was not going to be concerned with the possible reactions of Mildred and Augustus. The recent painful months had placed her out of sympathy with family drones who considered that the ties of blood entitled them to scoop up everything left by cleverer—and older—members of the family who had built up the fortune by virtue of their own efforts and brains. Let Mildred and Augustus look after themselves. Mrs. Abercrombie was her patient, and she was going to do anything in her power to foster any association that might make Mrs. Abercrombie happy.

"Er . . . have any of you heard the rumour . . ." As all eyes turned to him, Fr. Service faltered momentarily, then pressed on with the kind of gossip he was more comfortable with. "That we're going to be late getting to port? They say—I was talking with one of the crew—that they've gone off course to try to get away from this storm. If they don't get back on course again soon, it may add anything from twelve to twenty-four hours to our time."

"I don't think we *can* get away from this storm," Gloria said. "I think it's adopted us. Where we go—it goes. All the way to home port."

Across the dining salon, a woman pushed back her chair, stood irresolutely for a moment, then, fingertips pressed tightly to her mouth, headed unsteadily for the exit.

They really *did* go green around the gills, Val thought, watching her sympathetically. The woman had a sweep of pale green from cheekbone to jawline, just in front of her ears—where gills would be situated in an amphibious creature. And there must have been plenty of passengers aboard who wished they *were* amphibians tonight.

"She should never have attempted the soup," Mrs. Abercrombie pronounced severely as the door swung shut behind the unfortunate woman.

Dick Slade chuckled appreciatively, his eyes lingering on the doorway, as though he had enjoyed the sight of someone else's intense discomfort. Or, perhaps, in thankfulness that he had not been the one to make such an ignominious exit in public.

"Our expert, here—" Dick Slade turned to the couple newly-arrived at the adjoining table and brought them into the picture, indicating Mrs. Abercrombie— "our expert recommends the fish."

"Plain," Mrs. Abercrombie agreed. "No sauces."

"That sounds all right to me," Susan said, and her companion murmured agreement.

The waiter noted their order, his expression a curious mixture, which seemed to be compounded partly of relief and congratulation that his tables were taking care of themselves, and partly of a natural dismay at the thought of facing a temperamental chef and imparting once again the information that his best efforts were being disdained by ungrateful passengers. He moved away from the table slowly, then the floor tilted under his feet, sending him in running steps towards the kitchen.

She hoped the brakes on Mrs. Abercrombie's wheelchair held. Automatically, Val put out a hand to one of the wheels and tried to move it; it stood firm. It had seemed too perilous to attempt to transfer Mrs. Abercrombie from the wheelchair into an upright chair with the sea behaving so erratically beneath them. Although the wheelchair left her at a slightly lower level than might be entirely comfortable for eating, it was safer than having to worry about her balancing in an ordinary dining chair. So far, it appeared to be all right.

"Don't fuss so!" Mrs. Abercrombie hissed, in a sharp aside. "It's perfectly satisfactory."

Val drew her hand away quickly. It had been tactless of her to call any additional attention to Mrs. Abercrombie's plight. The presence of the wheelchair was enough. Combined with her adamant refusal to change out of uniform, it spotlighted Mrs. Abercrombie as one who had faltered and fallen in the battle for health. One who needed constant medical help and supervision to regain a position the people around her had never lost.

Not the light any woman would choose to be seen in— especially with a new admirer in the offing.

Val sighed under her breath, foreseeing new arguments with Mrs. Abercrombie over the old issue: Mrs. Abercrombie was determined to leave the ship under her own steam. Val contested that the day they docked would be the day the wheelchair would be most needed. Mrs. Abercrombie could not possibly stand for the time it would take to clear Immigration, Customs, and then the long wait for transport. The strain would undo all the good that had been accomplished, it might even bring on another attack.

Once ashore, however, it would be a different matter. Then she would allow Mrs. Abercrombie to slowly abandon the wheelchair. Just for a few hours a day, at first, the time gradually increasing as her strength increased. Idly, she wondered whether Mrs. Abercrombie would have to get her land legs back like the rest of them, or whether, not having used her legs at all aboard ship, Mrs. Abercrombie would have less trouble than she in walking normally during the first few days.

Once ashore, she would even put aside her uniform. Pack it away until it was needed again—until she decided whether she would go on nursing after the case was settled. She would wear one of the pretty drip-dry dresses she had packed and not thought about for weeks. That would please Mrs. Abercrombie. Then there would be nothing to mark her as an invalid. She would be just another American tourist, occasionally leaning heavily on the arm of the girl with her—a daughter, or niece, perhaps. Without the uniform, she would not be immediately identifiable as a paid nurse-companion. That alone would do wonders for Mrs. Abercrombie's morale. And she, too, would feel better, knowing that she could resume her own identity in a foreign country where no one would be covertly watching, knowing all about her, wondering whether or not she were really guilty as accused.

Once ashore . . .

The waiter returned with a tray bearing covered dishes and began dealing out their portions, working his way around the table as speedily as he could. Was it through skill or just good luck that the food landed into their plates rather than their laps? Both, probably. With the ship skittering about like this, it would take more than skill to balance against each unexpected movement.

There was something reassuring about the look of the unadorned fish and mashed potatoes. Like a nursery tea, it seemed bland and yet not unappetizing—something uncertain stomachs could reasonably cope with.

The others seemed to feel that way, too. Dick Slade had no hesitation about picking up his fork and beginning. And yet, perhaps he should have hesitated.

Val glanced uneasily at the cleric in their midst. Although she had noticed him in the background, this was the first time she had seen him at close quarters. He had joined them at their table with a murmured word to Gloria—the only other of their regular tablemates who was present tonight. Gloria, of course, had had to invite him to join them. His own table being empty, it would have seemed unfriendly, perhaps anti-clerical, not to.

Should they, perhaps, have invited Fr. Service to say grace? Or was it up to him to assert himself and impose grace upon them before they began eating?

Fr. Service, however, had picked up his fork almost as soon as Dick Slade and was now eating thoughtfully, seemingly unaware of any social nuances. Had he dipped his own head silently for a moment—or was it just the motion of the ship that had given that impression? If it were difficult for those around him, it surely must be twice as difficult for him, always treading the tightrope between the believers and the unbelievers, anxious not to embarrass or offend either, yet with inevitable awkwardness all along the way.

"Do you really think we're going to be *very* late getting into port?" Gloria had been thinking. She had never yet arrived without finding a contingent of relatives waiting to meet her. Some of them came quite long distances—and they wouldn't have budgeted for an extra night or two, just hanging around in hotels waiting for the ship to come in.

"Too soon to say." Dick Slade broke in while Fr. Service was still measuring his reply. "It would all depend on how much time they can make up. If they take a longer route, but go faster, then it shouldn't make much difference at all. *They* won't want to waste time, either, you know. They have their schedules to maintain."

"But, if it *should* take longer," Gloria insisted. "What do they do about it? I mean, do they have ways of letting people know? The ones who are going to meet the ship, I mean?"

"They haven't even let *us* know yet," Dick Slade said. "Not officially."

"It may be nothing but a rumour," Mrs. Abercrombie said firmly. "Shipboard is a great place for rumours. It's like being in an enclosed, hothouse community—everything grows faster and larger than life, even while you're looking at it."

"I *said* it was a rumour," Fr. Service defended hastily. "I heard it from one of the crew, but that doesn't necessarily mean—"

"The worst rumours—or the best—always start on the shop floor," Dick Slade said. "I'll bet you it would beat shipboard as a rumour factory any day in the week."

"But there may be some truth in—"

They were all talking at once now, animated by the problems that might lie ahead. They ate abstractedly, automatically, no longer worried about seasickness. Which was the best way to avoid it, Val thought. Not that she had any fears for Mrs. Abercrombie on that score, but one or two of the others had looked as though they might fall by the wayside with any encouragement. Keeping their minds off the possibility was the best ounce of prevention.

"Of course, I don't *have* to be anywhere at any particular time," Dick Slade said, a trifle regretfully. "That's one of the things about retirement—you can go at your own pace. But what about my hotel reservations? Will they know what's happened? I'd hate to get there next day and find they hadn't kept my room."

"Won't it be in the papers?" Susan leaned over from the next table, caught up in their conversation.

"Why should it be?" her own companion wanted to know. "This may seem a big thing to us, but it's probably just the usual Atlantic storm. Nothing has happened so far that would rate us any headlines."

"Let's hope nothing does!" The words were torn from Val, her shudder was genuine, but too exaggerated for the subject matter under discussion. She saw Dick Slade's eyes resting on her speculatively and tried to pull herself together. Why confirm what he already suspected—or knew? But the thought of headlines—more headlines—of reporters and photographers on the pier, waiting to meet the ship, to get interviews, pictures—She put down her fork and clasped her hands together tightly in her lap until they stopped shaking.

"We *all* have hotel reservations," Mrs. Abercrombie said. "If there isn't a small paragraph in the papers, I should expect the hotels to keep the rooms as a matter of course. After all, so many people travel by air these days—and there seem to be twice as many delays in air travel. Airports are always being closed down by fog or bad weather and planes diverted to other cities. It must make things rather difficult for hoteliers, but they must be used to it by now."

"Thank God we're *not* up in this in a plane tonight!" Gloria laughed nervously. "This is bad enough—but can

101

you imagine the way we'd be tossed around in the air? And with nothing underneath us."

This time everyone shuddered, then looked around, exchanging glances of mutual congratulation. Their situation indeed could have been a lot worse.

The *Beatrice Cenci* hopscotched another wave, and they looked uncertain again.

It wasn't too bad, Susan thought, so long as you kept your eyes off the carafe of water in the centre of the table. That endlessly moving water, relentlessly sloping up the side of the carafe, hesitating, then sliding back and crawling up the opposite side, hesitating at high point, sliding back—She pulled her eyes away, tried to concentrate on an immovable point, on something that would not be a reminder of the constant motion of the ship and the ocean beneath it.

"Are you all right?" Professor Cook was watching her with some concern.

"I think so." She smiled, a bit shakily, and tried not to look at the water carafe. Not if she wanted to remain all right.

"You're sure?"

"Yes, thank you, Prof—"

"I thought you were going to call me Ben," he cut in. "We agreed on that earlier."

"Ben." She tried to focus on his face, but that seemed to be swaying erratically, too. She blinked and tried again.

"See here, have you taken anything?"

"Anything?"

"Sealegs? Kwells? Any kind of dramamine? If not, you'd better. I've got some here—" He pulled a small packet of tablets out of his pocket, offering them to her.

"No!" Her rejection was instinctive, automatic, born of too many memories of too many medications forced on her when she was lying helpless waiting for the bones to knit. Pain-killers that sent her into a twilight world of nightmares.

"Go on," he urged. "Take two. It will make all the difference. You won't have to worry after that."

"No. No, thank you. I—I hate taking things."

"There's nothing wrong with them, I assure you." He looked surprised—and a little offended. "They're just dramamine. Take one, anyway. If you're not used to them, that will probably do the trick."

"No, please." She shrank away, some indefinable change in his attitude repelling her as much as the tablets.

"Come on," he urged, smiling. "It won't hurt you."

It was something about the quality of his smile, too eager, too ingratiating. Like Eric's, when he was intent on charming some victim into allowing him his own way.

"I'm sorry—" She pushed back her chair. "I think I ought to go back to my cabin and lie down."

"But you haven't finished your dinner."

She looked at the remaining fish and a faint queasiness stirred and uncurled itself through her stomach. "I've had enough."

"But you *will* be all right—?" He was on his feet, too, staring at her anxiously. "In the morning, I mean?"

"I hope so." Irritation gripped her at the thought of being expected to guarantee her condition some twelve hours hence.

"I'm sorry." He responded apologetically to the curtness in her manner. "It was a silly thing to say. But I suddenly couldn't stand the thought that you might disappear into your cabin for the remainder of the voyage. After we've only just begun to know each other."

The *Beatrice Cenci* quivered beneath her feet and skipped over another wave. Otherwise her rejoinder might have been even brusquer than her last remark. Some men felt they were entitled to a shipboard romance as part of their ticket price. Others formed attachments as a way of prolonging the journey and postponing the moment when they found themselves strangers on an alien shore.

Whichever applied to Professor Benjamin Cook, she was not willing to be a party to it at the best of times. The *Beatrice Cenci* tilted, attempted to top a wave, and fell back into a trough. And this was not the best of times.

"I really must get back to my cabin." Susan took a care-

ful breath and started across the wide expanse of dining salon floor.

"You're sure it's the wise thing to do?" He was still at
her side, hovering, solicitous. "Wouldn't you like to take
another turn around the deck first? The air might do you
good."

"No, thank you." The idea was even less enticing than
that of the dramamine tablets. And Ben Cook was not
nearly so charming as he had seemed this afternoon.

"Well, if you're sure." He appeared to sense that he
was losing ground. "Perhaps it would be wiser to get a good
night's sleep. Then you ought to be all right in the morning."

"Perhaps." She began to feel that she would be considerably improved if he would only go away and leave her
alone.

"Well—" He opened the door for her and hesitated.

"You're quite sure—" Once more, he proffered the
dramamine tablets.

"No!—thank you." She moved away and left him standing there.

"*No*, thank you." Mrs. Abercrombie waved away the
waiter's half-hearted offer of dessert. He shrugged philo-
sophically and turned, without hope, to offer the menu to
the rest of her table companions.

"That's good enough for me." Dick Slade refused the
menu. "A word to the wise, as they say."

The others murmured agreement, content to have a
strong lead to follow. They watched Mrs. Abercrombie
hopefully, waiting for her reaction to the waiter's next suggestion, "Coffee?"

"*I* shan't," Mrs. Abercrombie declared. "Rather, I shall
have it brought to my stateroom." She smiled apologetically. "I'm afraid I'm a bit tired."

The tell-tale white line had come back to rim her lips
again, betraying the exertion the meal had cost her after all.
Val started up guiltily. She should have noticed. Mrs. Abercrombie was so good at dissembling where her health was

concerned that it was not surprising that she had successfully bluffed her way through dinner. It was true that Mrs. Abercrombie had probably genuinely enjoyed acting as hostess to the table, but it was unforgiveable for her nurse not to have realized the situation. This whole voyage, which had promised so much as a health restorer, was close to being a dismal failure. It was all right for doctors to prescribe an ocean voyage for their patient's health, but what they had in mind was a smooth sea, blue skies, a comfortable deck-chair, and hovering attendants—not an Atlantic storm and a ship that seemed at times to be trying to turn itself inside-out.

"Please. Allow me—" Before Val could resume the duties she had been so abruptly recalled to, Dick Slade was around the table and earnestly fumbling for the brake control of Mrs. Abercrombie's wheelchair. "I'll see you girls back to your cabin—it will be my privilege."

Mrs. Abercrombie began her familiar brushing-away gesture, then subsided, looking almost flattered. Val felt a sudden pang of foreboding. Looking at the two of them, no longer young, no longer in the best of health, she had the dismal feeling that the right thing might be happening— but for the wrong reasons.

Dick Slade—so recently bereft—was frowning in concentration as he manoeuvred the wheelchair free of the table and swung it out into the salon. He moved the chair smoothly now, gently, almost reverently, but there was a faraway look in his eye that was disquieting. He was with them—and yet he was not, the woman in the wheelchair was Mrs. Abercrombie—and yet she was not.

"I'll get the door—" But, again, before Val could dodge around the wheelchair to get to the door, she was thwarted. A beaming waiter stepped forward and flung the door open with a flourish for the wheelchair to pass through.

Val began to feel useless, and worse than useless, as though she were flapping around unnecessarily in their wake. She could disappear into the Borgia Bar or one of the public rooms and Mrs. Abercrombie and her escort would never notice. But would that be a wise thing to do?

She had the uneasy feeling that she had abruptly become the onlooker who sees most of the game. Or the proverbial fly on the wall; once again, seeing everything—but not liking what she saw one bit.

Her conviction grew that Dick Slade was obscurely trying to assuage some private grief and guilt by pretending to himself that Mrs. Abercrombie was the dead wife he had failed. There was more than casual politeness in the way he was leaning forward to murmur something to Mrs. Abercrombie as he pushed her down the long passageway. There was an extra solicitousness in the way he tried to balance the wheelchair against the roll of the ship.

Then Val heard him finish off a sentence with a swallowed, barely-articulated, "my dear," and she became certain. But what could she do about it? She would be accused of fantasizing herself were she to charge him with such a thing.

Perhaps he was not yet aware himself that he was doing it. Manufacturers were not notoriously abreast of psychological subtleties; the tricks a mind could play were not something that could be entered on a balance-sheet, therefore they were not worthy of notice unless they pushed some employee over the edge of sanity.

Perhaps he might not even think it very important. "What's it to you?" he might ask.

What *was* it to her if he could make himself feel a little better about the years of neglect to a devoted wife by now dancing attendance upon Mrs. Abercrombie? If he could ease his conscience a little by pretending, why shouldn't he?

Then Mrs. Abercrombie turned to say something to him. She was laughing, relaxed, the white rim had disappeared from around her lips.

But Dick Slade turned his head abruptly, as though his attention were urgently required somewhere else for just a moment. He did so with a faint frown which might have signified concentration rather than displeasure. But, by doing so, he avoided focusing on Mrs. Abercrombie; he avoided having his dream disturbed by the intrusion of a bright, live female personality—the wrong female personality.

And *that*, Val realized, was why it was her business. Mrs. Abercrombie could not know—*must* not know—that she was a stand-in for a dead woman.

Alicia Abercrombie had travelled a long way on the road to recovery. She had done it largely alone, beneath the indifferent gaze of Mildred and Augustus, and without the impetus to be received from someone close who really cared about her. She could make it on her own, of course— she had already proved that. Nevertheless, every additional bridge back to health and normality was to be applauded. Every thread, however tenuous, connecting her to the world was to be encouraged.

Unless it was a false thread, a broken reed—as Dick Slade threatened to be. That would not help her, that would be an absolute setback, perhaps triggering something worse.

No. Despite the sympathy she felt for Mr. Slade, Val looked critically at the scales and found him wanting. He must not be allowed to work out his own problems by using Mrs. Abercrombie. It was sad for him, perhaps—but it could be fatal for Mrs. Abercrombie.

And it was Mrs. Abercrombie, after all, she must care for and protect.

Chapter 11

Ships talk to themselves through the night, and the *Beatrice Cenci* was no exception. These long and stormy nights especially seemed to bring out the chatterbox in her. Her hull creaked. Unnumbered nuts and bolts sulked and snapped like unhappy couples discussing a trial separation—or perhaps a final parting. Inside fittings groaned protestations against being overloaded and undervalued—if they gave up the ghost and collapsed, where would the rest of the ship be?

Outside, the waves pounded against the hull, urgent, importuning, seeking entry. The foghorn still hooted a monotonous defiance, sounding weary of forever having to repeat the same bleak warning.

In the darkness, the cabin seemed to spin like a gyroscope, seeking a balance it had not yet attained, which might not be attainable. Not with the wind raging outside and the sea whipping itself into traitorous unsuspected whirlpools. They could call this a luxury liner until they were blue in the face but, in weather like this, it was still like shooting the rapids in a birch bark canoe. Your chances were probably just about as good, too.

Butler sat up in his bunk and snapped on the light. That helped a little. The strange night noises seemed to withdraw before the onslaught of light. Most of them. There was still a strange deep grumbling somewhere down in the guts of the ship. And a jittering clinking from the direction of the bathroom.

Butler wiped a film of perspiration from his forehead with the sleeve of his pyjamas. Why couldn't the bitch have chosen to fly the Atlantic like a normal civilized woman?

Then he could have picked her off at his leisure somewhere on the Continent.

It had seemed like a good idea at the beginning, but the trouble was that a ship was too small. If the weather had been better and he had been able to stay on deck, muffled up in a rug on a deck-chair, he would have felt happier. But that degree of anonymity had been wrested from him. Driven indoors by the weather, all the passengers were taking greater note of each other than they would otherwise have done. Constantly meeting in the shops, the public rooms, the bar, they had too much time on their hands, too much opportunity to study each other, speculate on each other's pasts, wonder about their future, notice who were pairing off together. It was a small town community magnified—or reduced—a hundredfold. The sort of place he thought he'd escaped from a long time ago.

Nerves! Butler threw back the coverings and stood up. He was getting jumpy because the time for action was getting close. Like an actor with first-night nerves.

Except that tomorrow wasn't the first night—it was the last night out. His move had to be made then, while the ship was still too far from shore for any radio call for help to bring out helicopters or rescue craft in time to be helpful.

Son-of-a-bitching weather! Butler began to pace the cabin. It all depended on getting her out on deck again. And who'd want to go out on deck in weather like this? He could persuade her to, of course, he was confident of that. The risk was in being seen to persuade her.

It was like being in the middle of a Spies' Convention. Everybody was watching you all the time—whether you noticed it or not. Worse, unseen ears were listening. Ears that were, inevitably, connected to some big mouth that later might start flapping, "She didn't *really* want to go out on deck, but that man kept on at her—"

The noise from the bathroom was like the steady chattering of teeth now. Butler whirled and darted for it, kicking the door open as though he expected to surprise an FBI man behind it. The door hit the wall and bounded back, then swung open, adding a gentle creaking noise to the other sounds.

After a moment, Butler traced the source of the chattering. The water glasses were jittering in their metal rings. He might have thought of that if he hadn't been so jittery himself.

He tore paper handkerchiefs from their holder and lifted out the glasses, padding the metal rings before he replaced them. That muffled the noise to the point where there would be silence once he'd closed the bathroom door again.

On second thought, he repossessed one of the glasses, splashed a bit of water into it, and carried it back into the cabin where he poured in a generous amount from his flask. That was better. Maybe he was overplaying his role, but he was beginning to feel like a teetotaller keeping down to the amount his companions were drinking before dinner.

No use going back to bed just yet. He sank into the armchair and tried to pretend it was a rocking-chair. That made the motion of the ship more acceptable. He could close his eyes and almost think he was somewhere else— except for that damned noise coming from down below. There was no shutting that out.

He took a deep pull at his drink and, almost imperceptibly, tightened muscles began to relax. That was more like it.

What was there to worry about, after all? His plans were foolproof. She trusted him. More—she would never dream of suspecting him in the first place. His cover was perfect. Why shouldn't it be? He had thrown himself into the role so wholeheartedly that there were moments when he even convinced himself.

Nothing could go wrong. Not here, not now. Perhaps ashore. But not on board the *Beatrice Cenci*—storm notwithstanding. She was a good ship, new, strong, seaworthy. There was nothing to worry about here.

On shore. Yes. On shore, treachery lurked. Back in New York, that was where the double-cross might be waiting. The double-cross, or the triple-cross, or the quadruple-cross. You couldn't trust any of them. That was why he carried insurance.

Yes, and let them all know that he carried it. Let every Christ-forsaken one of them know: if anything happened to him, if any one of them betrayed him, they were *all* in it—up to their eyeballs.

They hadn't liked it. None of them. He took another deep swallow and let the warmth spreading through his limbs tempt him into relaxing. They'd hated it. Why shouldn't they? If one of them got funny, they were *all* in the cart. That was the way it was, and that was the way it was going to stay. It was the only safe insurance.

While he was all right, they were all okay. If anything happened to him, they'd had it—every last one of them.

He'd figured it out long ago. While he was still working for the Syndicate. Watching the way they did things, learning from it. Improving it. Then, when branching out on his own, he'd started his own system.

And he'd operated it from the beginning, from the very first outside job. He'd kept a record of every contract: date, name of contractor, subject of contract, and the details of the job after it had been accomplished—right down to the tiniest point. So that the police, in case the record ever had cause to come into their hands, would realize that he knew what he was talking about, that it was not some kind of elaborate hoax. They'd be stunned and disbelieving at first, but they'd have to check the information out. As every detail tallied, case after case, they'd be forced into belief—and then into action. Against those who were still alive, the ones who had put out the contracts.

Against the final wise guy—the one who'd thought Butler was bluffing and had betrayed him. That wise guy would be the first one they landed on. Butler ensured that by carrying details of the current contract with him until it was executed. In case of betrayal, that would be the first to be found—and, with it, information on where to find the master file.

Yeah, but it wasn't very likely. He sank the rest of that drink and got up to pour himself another. That was the point of the whole operation. He made sure all his clients knew about that file. That was why it was insurance.

It insured that the client *didn't* betray him. Better than that—it insured that he dealt only with genuine clients. He was passed from one to another, and the old ones warned the new ones—although he found ways of dropping a mention of the file himself. Just in case it had been forgotten or, rather, overlooked. No one was going to forget a thing like that. Not when it was *his* neck in a noose.

It insured that he was only referred to other genuine clients.

The police never closed their books on murder. The Statute of Limitations didn't apply to murder.

So the client knew—no matter how long ago he had taken out the contract—that the police would still be interested. Would still be looking him up if those records ever came into their hands.

It was a long chain, going quite a way back now. But, as every one of them knew, a chain depended on its weakest link. And that was why he could relax—the links were all watching each other, knowing their safety depended on the strength of each one.

Why, any one of them would kill the link that threatened to betray him. So long as he was safe, they were all safe.

Undoubtedly every one of them would like to see him dead. But they knew the penalty for that. His microfilmed file was in an unknown place—the only thing certain about it was that they were recorded in it, and that it would be turned over to the police if he died in any mysterious way. If he died at all.

Maybe, long years hence, if he decided to retire, he might destroy those records. By then, he would probably be safe. The clients were mostly older, or the same age, as himself. Those who were younger would presumably have more things to interest them than worrying about an incident in their past. The younger ones were tougher—more ruthless, more ready to trust their own judgement—or luck. Less ready to believe in the omniscience of the cops, the pigs, the fuzz. For them, the spell was broken. They knew a cop could be bought, could be damaged, could be—if necessary—killed.

No, the young ones weren't the ones to worry about. And he knew how to keep the others in line.

So what was the point of nerves? It was all foolproof. And, day after tomorrow, he'd roll off the ship and disappear. Safe in a foreign country. Unsuspected. Free to go his own way, be a tourist, see the sights, and—eventually—go back Stateside and pick up another contract when the money ran low.

It was a sweet set-up. He raised his glass to it: *Tomorrow and tomorrow and tomorrow.*

Roll on the dawn.

Chapter 12

There was one thing to be thankful for. Guido had slept like a log all night. He was still sleeping. He was a real "rocked in the cradle of the deep" baby, all right. He looked ready to go on sleeping for hours yet.

And why shouldn't he? Back home, it was the middle of the night. She ought to be sound asleep herself, except that she'd hardly slept at all. It was now six o'clock in the morning according to shipboard time—tonight they'd put their clocks ahead one last hour and that would be it. They'd be on European time. Eventually, their stomachs and reflexes would catch up with their watches. But it was still better than doing it in one great gulp on a jet flight.

She closed her eyes experimentally, and opened them again. It was no good, she was wide awake. Groggy, but wide awake. And, if she got up and began moving around the stateroom, she'd wake up Guido. That would mean he wouldn't go back to sleep again, either, but would be fretful for the rest of the day.

On the other hand, she couldn't bear to just lie awake in her bunk. She was too alive—too restless. She might as well be up and doing something.

It would probably be all right to leave Guido by himself for a short time. She could stop off and speak to the stewardess to make sure he was looked in at occasionally. And she could come back to the stateroom herself every little while and check on him. It ought to be all right.

Gloria dressed slowly, still with the underwater feeling fatigue gave her. She hadn't felt so tired for a long time—not since those last days of pregnancy, just before Guido was born. And then Lorenzo had been there to help. He'd been almost a different person during those days, so sweet, so thoughtful, so very careful of her.

She shook her head, dismissing memories, denying dreams, affirming the present. She was here and now. On board the *Beatrice Cenci*, one day—or maybe two days—out of Genoa, and it was quarter past six in the morning.

Furthermore, it looked like a sunny morning. A golden sliver of light showed at the porthole. She crossed and moved the curtain fractionally to look out.

It *was* sunshine. The sea a crisp cold blue, still moving erratically beneath the ship, but clear. Perhaps they had outsailed the storm.

Feeling more light-hearted, she tiptoed across to the bathroom to put her make-up on. Even if it were as cold as it looked outside, it would still make a big difference to be able to sit on deck this morning. There was no denying a certain beleaguered feeling had set in over the past few days. The prospect of open deck and a deck-chair seemed a sudden unhoped-for glimpse of a new freedom. Guido would enjoy it, too.

She wiped off her lipstick and started again. The ship was still living a life of its own, communing with the waves, independent of the passengers. The passengers had learned to beware during the past few days, they should not forget their hard-learned lessons just because the sun was shining.

Steadying herself against the wash-basin, Gloria managed to apply the lipstick within a reasonable proximity to her natural lipline this time. They might have outsailed the storm but, obviously, they had not yet outrun the eddying waves from it. There was still a bit more running to be done.

She snapped off the light and went back into the cabin, checking automatically to see that Guido was still deep in slumber. He was, and she felt a sudden thrill of freedom. She could actually leave him here and go out on deck alone. Go anywhere on the ship, in fact, exulting in the luxury of being by herself.

Except—At the doorway, she paused thoughtfully. Where was there to go at this hour? That was the catch. You might know there'd always be a catch. It was only half past six—a. m. Social events were a bit thin on the ground at this hour. If only Guido would be more co-operative and conk out at a decent hour in the afternoon or early evening, she might be able to take some real advantage of the freedom. Sit in on a bridge game, maybe. Or go to a movie, or dance, or something equally wild. But he was just like his father— determined to keep an eye on her during every waking moment.

Oh, well. She shrugged, closing the door softly behind her. There was one event you could always find on board ship at an ungodly hour like this . . .

The deck rose to meet her knee as she genuflected and the unexpectedly sharp impact brought a blur of tears to her eyes. She caught at the back of one of the smoking-room chairs to steady herself, and remained in a kneeling position while the pain cleared. Above her head, she heard the murmured dialogue of the morning Mass continuing in an uninterrupted ageless flow.

Then the words began to register and she was conscious of a faint surprise. Somehow, she had not had the impression that Fr. Service spoke Italian.

She raised her head. The celebrant was bowing over the chalice. He raised his own head suddenly and looked out over his sparse congregation, seeming faintly surprised to see anyone there at all. As well he might be at that hour of the morning.

He was short and bearded—definitely not Fr. Service. She hadn't seen him before—he must have come up from Tourist. Fr. Service was probably taking the 7:15 Mass then.

Which brought up a neat little crisis of conscience. Shipboard priests hoarded their nominal parishioners like misers, and exerted a moral blackmail. Unspoken, it was made known that loyalty and fealty were expected—which was to say that any one of them contemplating going to Mass had better attend *his* Mass—no matter what terrifying hour it was scheduled for.

Well, she'd tried. But it had turned out to be the wrong Mass. Nor could she tiptoe out and try coming back for the 7:15. She had already been spotted as one of the flock—standing out sharply as the only passenger among the members of the crew who had dropped in on their release from the night watches.

So, that meant a quick getaway at the end of Mass, before she got caught in the vicinity by Fr. Service and found herself expected to stay on through *his* Mass. And she didn't want to leave Guido alone that long—even supposing she felt like attending two Masses in a row.

But the old boy kept on going—for a terrible moment, she thought he was even going to indulge in a sermon. He seemed to realize that it wasn't quite the done thing on shipboard and checked himself with visible reluctance. Nevertheless, he took his time over everything else. Perhaps he was trying to fill in until first breakfast.

Guiltily, Gloria began a kneeling backward shuffle, aiming towards the doorway. Nor was she the only restless member of the congregation; several of the crew were looking at their watches and making *sotto voce* noises of distress and displeasure. Under cover of rising, some of them sidled closer to the exit.

The priest attempted to transfix them with a glare, to shame them with a muttered remark which, denuded of its heavy accent, was obviously meant to be. "Will ye not watch one hour with me?"

Unfortunately, it was too close to the truth. Too many of them were already suspecting that he intended to go on for an hour. It could not be allowed, some had to go on duty, there were tasks to be done. A ship did not run by itself.

The ship's nurse was the first to leave, every crisp starched inch of her uniform whispering of important matters to be seen to, of temporal works of mercy to be achieved. Who could dare gainsay her? A faint sigh of envy drifted in the wake of her passage.

The crew member serving as altar boy did his best. With defensive glances at his colleagues, as though to prove it was not *his* fault, he threw the responses back at the priest so quickly that he sometimes cut off the end of the priest's line. It was a good try, and speeded things up a little—but not enough.

Finally, with a reluctant sigh, the old padre faced them and admitted, "The Mass is ended." They tripped over one another as, muttering a heartfelt "Grazie Dio," they leaped for the outside world. His reproachful look followed them.

Too late. Gloria's heart sank as she nearly collided with the dark figure lurking outside the smoking-room door, waiting his turn to say Mass. She looked up quickly, framing excuses which faded as she saw his face.

He was not Fr. Service. She smiled vaguely and side-stepped. There was a notice pinned beside the smoking-room door. She had glanced at it on her way in. Now, puzzled, she read it more carefully. The wording remained the same. "Masses: 6:30 a.m.; 7:15 a.m."

"But—" Turning, she found the "altar boy," also desperate to escape, lest he be press-ganged into serving at the second Mass, as well. She caught at his sleeve, delaying him, to ask her question.

"But, what about Father Service? When does he say *his* Mass?"

"Scusi?" The "altar boy" shrugged, looking nervously over his shoulder into the smoking room, where the newly-arrived priest was already laying out his vestments and staring meaningly for help.

"The third priest," Gloria clarified. "Where is he today? He isn't seasick, is he?"

"No, no." Firmly, he detached her hand and moved away. "Is no third priest. No. Very unusual. We only carry two priests this voyage."

Susan slid the blanket up closer around her ears and inhaled deeply. The fresh crisp sea air, faintly tanged with disinfectant from the early morning scrubbing down of the decks, *was* bracing. She *did* feel better up on deck.

She repeated the thought firmly to herself, thankful to just lie back and find that her equilibrium was not so disturbed as it had been. There was a sporting chance that this was where the expression "Take it lying down" had come from. The incessant motion of the ship, which seemed to pull and drag at one when upright, was definitely less unsettling when spread over a wider area, such as one presented when lying back in a deck-chair. It was only unfortunate that the weather had not been more conducive to deck-chair relaxation throughout the earlier part of the voyage.

A rattle of crockery sounded at the far end of the deck where a serving trolley was being wheeled out. Susan closed her eyes against it. Perhaps if they thought she was asleep they would pass by and not attempt to inflict their bouillon on her. She had had a cup of tea and some dry toast in her cabin. That was quite enough.

Determinedly she kept her eyes closed as she felt the considering gaze sweeping over her face. She sensed the deck steward's hesitation beside her chair. He had served the nearest passengers, but the deck-chairs on either side of her were empty. Once he got past her, she would be safe from his undesired solicitude.

It was rather hard lines on him, of course. With the weather having been so frightful, he hadn't been able to do much to earn his tips. Today was his last chance to make sure his passengers were properly aware of him. Patently, he was now weighing up whether it would be better to wake the signorina for her bouillon, or whether she would better appreciate being left to undisturbed repose.

Farther along the row of deck-chairs, someone coughed impatiently. With a faint sigh, the deck steward bowed to the inevitable and continued down towards the more demanding passengers. It was to be hoped that the signorina would not resent being left out when she awakened, but shipboard life abounded in such small crises and one had to be philosophical about it. In any case, he brightened, there was still afternoon tea.

Susan relaxed as she heard the trolley roll safely past. The warmth of the sun seemed to increase with every minute as they sailed southwards, although the few miles they had covered since her coming on deck could not possibly make that much difference. The sea air was still chill and she was glad she had the blanket. Some of the hardier souls had thrown off their blankets—but that was their imaginations at work.

Cautiously, she risked opening one eye a narrow slit, like a wary cat spying out the terrain before admitting it was awake. The trolley had turned the corner now and she could hear the diminishing rattle as it proceeded along the starboard length of the ship.

The coast clear, she opened both eyes, blinking reflectively. All clear. The deck immediately before her was clear to the railing. Safe.

"PROVIDED ALWAYS . . ." It swooped at her again, as it always did when she was tired, unguarded. *The sick thought*. When she was rested, healthy, it never came to bother her. Then she knew that Eric was doing well enough, that he was slowly—very slowly, without the backing he so desperately wanted, if not needed—working his way upward in the field he loved. He would never actually try that trick again—it had been a childish aberration, a mad, uncalculated throw of the dice, once tried, never to be repeated. An unsuccessful attempt on her life now would cost him everything he had so painstakingly gained—everything he still hoped to achieve.

"*Provided always* . . ." it was a sick thought. She breathed deeply, closing her eyes, her mind, against it, trying to banish it back to the realm of nightmare, where it belonged.

"*There* you are!" It was a voice, a presence, she could not close her mind against. It was in front of her—real, present. "You nearly missed your bouillon—but it's all right. I've got it for you."

There was a clank, a scrape of pottery and an intrusive smell of a faintly greasy, faintly acid (as of unripe tomatoes) concoction almost immediately beneath her nose.

She opened her eyes again reluctantly. Benjamin Cook stood beside her, two cups of bouillon—crackers perched against them in the saucers—in his hands.

"They went right past you," he said. "They must have thought you were asleep."

"I was," she lied.

"It's all right." He set the cup and saucer down perilously on the arm of her deck-chair. "I've seen to it that you weren't left out."

The viscous liquid moved with the motion of the ship. Up and down, up, up and nearly over the rim. Then sinking back and slowly climbing up the opposite side. Up and down.

She pulled her eyes away. "You shouldn't have bothered." Up and down . . . "I didn't really want any."

"Why not?" He was affronted, immediately defensive. "You've paid for all this, you know."

"That doesn't mean I have to have it." She could tell by his bewildered, still faintly affronted look that such a concept was beyond him.

"You've paid for it," he said again. "There's no sense in letting it go to waste."

"You may be right." She appeared to give in gracefully, taking the saucer and setting it down on the deck beside her chair. With any luck, the *Beatrice Cenci* might give one of her unheralded lurches and spill the bouillon so that she would not have to ingest it and yet honour would be satisfied.

"Drink it up," he urged, gulping at his own. "It will do you good."

She couldn't imagine that for a moment. "It was very kind of you," she said, "but I don't really think I could cope with it. Why don't you have it?"

"Oh no." He lowered his cup in consternation. "I couldn't do that. It's yours."

"But if I don't want it, surely I can give it to you?" His vehemence amused her.

"It's not the same thing at all. You ought to have it. You didn't finish your meal last night, did you? And what did you have for breakfast this morning? Not bacon and eggs, I'll bet."

"No, not that." She closed her eyes against the vision. "But I had quite as much as I wanted."

In the abrupt silence, she opened her eyes to see how this had registered. She was just in time to see the horizon swoop into view as, to the accompaniment of a heavy grinding noise from somewhere deep inside her, the *Beatrice Cenci* lurched down into the trough of a wave. Almost immediately, there followed the light clatter she had been hoping to hear. She saw the bouillon spill across the deck towards the gutter beneath the ship's rail.

"What was that?" Ben Cook had gone pale.

"I'm afraid that was my bouillon." Why should it upset him so much?

"No—no, I didn't mean that." He looked around uneasily. "I mean that awful noise the ship keeps making. Like a ghastly metallic groan—it was doing it all night. Every time I started to doze off, it would make that noise again." He looked at her incredulously. "Do you mean to say you didn't notice it?"

"Oh, that. Yes, I did. It's nothing to worry about. Ships always make what seems to be a lot of noise during stormy nights. This *is* your first sea voyage, isn't it?"

"Yes. Yes, it is." He was ready to be offended by her amusement, but the *Beatrice Cenci* heeled abruptly in the other direction and he lost his balance, sitting down heavily on the footrest of her deck-chair.

"You mean this sort of thing happens often?" He glanced skywards, as though regretting not being aloft.

"This is worse than usual," she admitted. "At least, I think it is. I haven't travelled at this time of the year before, but they say we're catching bits of hurricane weather."

With the shuddering metallic groan again, the *Beatrice Cenci* heeled back on to the level and proceeded on an even keel.

"What *is* that noise?" He was not to be diverted by the weather. "It sounds as though it's coming from directly under us. What's down there?"

"It's the hold," she said. "Where they stow the cargo. You saw them loading when we boarded, didn't you?"

"Yes." He was suddenly reflective. "Heavy loading—lots of crates of heavy machinery, even some automobiles. I remember thinking then that it didn't look safe."

"It's perfectly safe," Susan said, with a touch of asperity. She wondered what his pupils called him. Possibly, in his own classroom he would have more authority, but it was hard to picture him in charge of pupils. She wondered if he could control them adequately, or whether his was one of those classrooms from which uproar could be heard for a great deal of the time, quelled only when a headmaster or more senior teacher opened the door.

"Oh, I suppose it must be." He sounded unconvinced. "But something could still go wrong, couldn't it? The ship seems to have taken a heavy battering during the past few days. It's been quite a storm."

"And I only hope it's over." The deck had developed a suspicious quiver, as though forces were thudding up through the hull from fathoms beneath it. "We haven't changed course again, have we? We seem to be sailing back into it."

"Or perhaps we've sailed through it—the eye of the hurricane, as it were—and are coming out into the turbulence on the other side."

"Surely we must be too close to land for that?" She looked at him, but there was no trace of a smile on his face. He had meant it quite seriously.

"I don't know. Perhaps we are. It's the last night out. We'll be in Italy tomorrow night." He gazed hopefully at the horizon.

"Have you heard anything about our arrival time?" If he had been roaming about the ship all morning, he might have picked up the latest rumours.

"Ah, yes. They still aren't sure. We were originally due in late afternoon, but I gather early evening is more likely now. They've been trying to make up for lost time." He glanced down at the deckboards unhappily. "Perhaps that's why we've been hearing all the noise—they've been exceeding their speed limit."

She tried not to laugh, but lost the battle. Curiously, it didn't seem to upset him this time. "I've said something terribly un-nautical again?" He smiled resignedly. "It doesn't really matter. I'd already planned to fly home at the end of my sabbatical. I don't expect I'll ever travel by ship again. It isn't really my style."

"You've just had a very bad crossing. It would be a shame to let it put you off. I'm sure you would have enjoyed it tremendously if only the sea had been smoother and you could have spent more time on deck."

"That goes for you, too, I guess," he said. "You don't seem to have enjoyed the past couple of days very much. Are you coming up on deck again this afternoon?"

"Yes," she said. "I rather think I will. It seems a shame to waste a sunny afternoon at the film show."

"I'll see you up here after lunch then." He stooped and collected her cup and saucer, righting the cup and gazing consideringly at the few spoonfuls of liquid remaining at the bottom.

For an insane moment, she thought he was going to insist that she try to drink them. "I'm quite looking forward to lunch," she said hastily, hoping to forestall him. "I'm beginning to get my appetite back."

"That's good." He nodded at her, then strode over to the railing and tossed the remains of the bouillon and soggy crackers over the side. "We'll have tea up here on deck this afternoon."

"I'll wear my blue silk tonight," Mrs. Abercrombie directed. "And my pearls." She had been on the sun deck for a while during the morning and some colour had come into her face, giving her not only a healthier look but a younger one.

Was it solely due to a healthy morning on deck, Val wondered uneasily, or to the prospect of dazzling Dick Slade at the Gala Dinner tonight?

"What are you going to wear?" Mrs. Abercrombie demanded. "You aren't going to insist on that uniform tonight, are you? *Not* for the Gala Dinner."

"Well . . ." Val hesitated. She had been on the ship safely for nearly a week. If anyone suspected anything, they couldn't prove it. She was rather tired of the uniform herself; it was time to start being a private person again.

"All right. I'll wear my long black dress for the dinner—no uniform. In fact," she smiled at Mrs. Abercrombie, "no more uniform from now on."

"Really?" Mrs. Abercrombie looked as though she had been given a delightful and unexpected present. "You promise?"

"I promise." Val held out her hand and Mrs. Abercrombie grasped it eagerly, beginning to pull herself upright with it. But the *Beatrice Cenci* dipped and reared suddenly, throwing Mrs. Abercrombie back into the wheelchair.

"Oh!" Furiously, impatiently, Mrs. Abercrombie struck the arm of the wheelchair with the flat of her hand. "And— once we're ashore—no more wheelchair, either." She looked up and beamed at Val. "*I* promise."

"It's a deal," Val said, lapsing into the phrase she had heard so often during her time in the mid-West and immediately regretting it. It brought back that time all too vividly.

"It is," Mrs. Abercrombie agreed. "And now I think I'll lie down and rest for a while. Why don't you run along and enjoy yourself. I'll be all right by myself."

She would, Val knew. Despite the bad crossing and being confined indoors, Mrs. Abercrombie had unquestionably improved. She had gained, or perhaps regained, some quality which had been missing before. Possibly a vitality which had been vitiated by the solemn and overly reverential visitations of Mildred and Augustus. Even Val had felt drained and depressed after Mildred and Augustus had made one of their tiptoeing exits, their hushed whispers assuring her mendaciously that "Aunt Alicia is looking simply splendid."

Perhaps, like herself, what Mrs. Abercrombie had most needed was the chance, and the time, to be a private person again.

"I'll go down to the Gift Galleries," Val decided. "There's still some shopping I'd like to do." A surge of exultation lifted her spirit. No more uniform, no more playacting. There was a lovely silk dress, printed in stained-glass colours, horrendously expensive—But no more pretending she couldn't afford expensive things, either. She was on her way to being a private person again—and that dress typified the sort of persona she was going to have, the life she was going to live from now on.

"I'll see you later," she said, heading for the door eagerly, not even noticing Mrs. Abercrombie's amused smile.

Chapter 13

It was just as well the voyage was nearly over—little Guido would have been spoiled rotten if it went on much longer. He sat on the floor of the shop now, contentedly gnawing on a pice of nougat the salesgirl had given him, while his mother huddled in a corner with the manageress, deep in complicated conversation.

Val stepped round the child carefully. Dribbling nougat only slightly, he grinned up at her. A charmer, even at that age. She smiled back at him, but continued on her way, doubting both their abilities at any more vocal communication.

In the rack against the far wall, she saw the dress, a fold of the skirt shimmering, drawing her like the warmth of a hearth fire on a cold day. She took it off the rack, gathering it to her hungrily. There were two or three others she liked, as well; she might as well try them all on while she was here. If she really liked them, she could buy them. She could afford them. Rather, she had passed beyond the point where she had to consider the cost of things. For the first time she was beginning to let her mind admit that thought, play with it, begin to realize what it could mean.

Before this, she had been too busy counting up what it had cost her personally.

"This way, signorina." Too well trained to shrug, the salesgirl permitted her eyebrows only the tiniest flicker as she glanced from the starched white uniform to the expensive dresses. "You need any help?"

"Thank you, I can manage." Val held the smile until the curtain had been swished shut, enclosing her in the minuscule fitting-room.

Slowly, luxuriously, she started with the least-favoured dress. Like most expensive garments, it presented an entirely different aspect one it was donned. Then the line and cut which had seemed negligible on the hanger came into their own, enveloping her with a chic for which almost anything could be forgiven—even the price.

Carefully she took it off and replaced it on the hanger, avoiding the price tag, trying to pretend to a conscience inured to years of penny-pinching and careful economies that she had not already made her decision.

It was a relief when the second dress was a disappointment. Hard to say precisely what was wrong with it, she just didn't like it. She glanced over her shoulder guiltily, almost expecting to find a censorious salesgirl frowning at her. Years of battling with English saleswomen—who could work themselves into a quivering fury if one rejected a dress that was ill-made and worse-fitting—had left a permanent guilt complex about refusing one that actually fitted perfectly on the flimsy grounds that you didn't like it.

But she was safe. No one stood there checking to see whether she were trying to escape her obligations. Quickly she put it back on its hanger and reached for *the* dress.

The most expensive of the lot. Naturally. And worth it. Bringing out nuances in her hair and skin tones that she had never known were there; hinting at an unsuspected richness in her figure; whispering, when she moved, of a grace and style that lesser mortals might never achieve. This was what every dress ought to be—yet so seldom was.

For a moment, for one fragile wistful moment, she wished that Ralphie could see her in it.

Too late, she tried to recall the thought. Memories came flooding back—all the memories she had so perilously been holding at bay since she came aboard the *Beatrice Cenci* . . .

The house on the hill. Isolated, windswept, yet well built, windows double-glazed, snug against the sub-zero temperatures and ice storms and blizzards of a mid-Western winter. Overlooking the town below, founded by the ancestors of its present occupants, strategically placed so that the townspeople had to look up to them. An attitude which persisted and was encouraged to this day.

And, in that house, the study. Warm and book-lined, on the ground floor, with french windows opening on to the sweep of velvet snow that was a flawless lawn in summer, commanding the view over the town and the surrounding plains.

The heart of the house. And, pulsing within that heart, the Grand Old Man.

Or, as Ralphie put it, "The Man Who Owned the Town." Old Horatio, her patient, the Grand Seigneur, the descendant of the Robber Barons, who had been there for so long that, by sheer longevity, he had made his ancestry respected, if not honoured.

The townspeople spoke of him in reverent undertones. The editor of the weekly paper called before printing one of his famous hard-hitting editorials to make sure he wasn't striking out at any targets that might not be approved.

And, filling the house around him, his loving relatives. At least, his relatives.

It was a big house, but they filled it, sometimes seeming to expand until they could have filled a house twice the size. That was when things were going well and they were in favour. When the Old Man was in a temper, they shrank into themselves until it seemed they might disappear. No imperative voices rang in the hallway, no orders were flung at the servants, no figure was so rash as to disturb the fallen giant, brooding in his den. The house might have been empty then.

"Sycophants, all of them!" he snarled. "Scared of their own shadows. And what about you, girl? Why are you still here? Aren't you afraid I'll bite you? Grrr! You see, you don't even jump. What's the matter, no human emotions? Do they teach you to pack them away when you put on that uniform?"

Hiding her smile, as she hid the precious moments she stole to lie back in Ralphie's arms, she remained cool under

129

fire. Once in a while, her amused tolerance broke through and, strangely, he did not seem to resent it.

"You've got guts. More guts than the whole lot of them put together. You're wasted, going on the way you are. Why in tarnation don't you—"

"Open wide, now. You know you've got to take it. Wider. Come on, now. That's it."

"Gaaargh! Filthy stuff! Marry me. Or let me adopt you. Whichever way you want it. Be sensible, Val."

"I *am* sensible. You're too old to marry, and I'm too old to adopt. Now your capsule. Come on, stop stalling. Open wide again. Be a good boy. That's it."

It had been their private joke. At least, she'd thought it had. Naturally, she'd never mentioned it to Ralphie or any of the others. The Old Man didn't mean it. But the others were too tense to have any sense of humour on any subject regarding the Old Man. Even Ralphie, for all his charm and self-assurance, jerked like a marionette when Horatio directed any remarks towards him.

How could she have guessed what was in the back of Horatio's mind? How could any of them? And, of course, none of them had.

When, smug and hovering like vultures, they gathered in the study after the funeral, she had joined them reluctantly, at the request of the family solicitor. She had expected only a token bequest, a small acknowledgement of the Old Man's gratitude for her care and friendship during the last eighteen months of his life. And, it was obvious, that was all the others expected for her.

As the enormity of the actual fact broke over them, one by one the heads turned to stare at her accusingly. Still stunned, she returned their gaze with a blank steadiness that was interpreted as arrogance, as challenge, as triumph, as anything but the unbelieving incredulity it actually was.

"We'll fight, of course." Ralphie's mother had broken the silence.

"Undue influence," one of the cousins agreed. "You only have to look at her. Taking advantage of a poor old man—"

If he had really been poor, no one would have cared. If he had been poor, none of them would have been there in the first place.

"No court in the world would uphold a Will like that," someone else said.

No court in this town, they meant. No court in this State.

"It's a valid Will," the solicitor defended. "Horatio was sound in mind, he knew what he was doing."

"You'd say that, of course," Ralphie's mother said. "I suppose we have you to thank for this."

"I drew up the Will, if that's what you mean." He had been the Old Man's lawyer. Now Val was aware that he had made his way to her side. Gravitating towards where the money was?

"I don't want—" she began. The lawyer's hand gripped her shoulder, stopping her.

"You don't want unpleasantness." Smoothly he changed the words she had intended to say. "Neither do any of us. When we have time to think it over, we'll realize that."

"Speak for yourself," the militant cousin said. "You're going to regret this as the worst day's work you ever did."

"I'll overlook that remark." The lawyer spoke in a tone of calm reasonableness. "This has been a very emotional day. We're all overwrought—"

Through it all, Ralphie had said nothing. The babble of voices rose and fell around him. Val waited for him to come to her and tell her that he understood, that he wasn't angry with her. But only the lawyer stood by her side.

Naturally, Ralphie was stunned, too. She tried to defend him, tried to hide from herself the molten fury that had burned in his eyes as the Will's key clause was read out. Since that time he had been actively avoiding her eyes.

"You needn't worry—" At her side, Lawyer Clements continued to pump encouragement into her unheeding ear. "They can't break the Will—it's watertight. They haven't a leg to stand on. *He* saw to that. They've been well enough provided for. A court won't have too much sympathy for them. They've got enough out of him. They thought they were going to get everything—that's their trouble. Sheer greed."

"I don't—"

"Greed, that's all." Again, he cut her off. "But Old Horatio saw it coming. He left a contingency fund so that we can fight them. And we'll win. It might take a little time, but we'll win in the end. You needn't have any fear about that."

The others had withdrawn to the far side of the room, talking in undertones now, marshalling their forces. Ralphie still hadn't looked at her. Although, she noticed with flickering hope, he was standing slightly apart from the others, as though not quite committed to their cause.

"I don't want the money," she said.

"Naturally that's your first reaction," the lawyer soothed. "Horatio thought it would be. That's why I have my orders. I'm to stand by you and not let you sign anything until you've had a chance to think it over. He *wanted* you to have the money, you know. In a sense, you owe it to him to take it. You know what he thought of the others. Even so, he left them enough to keep a Judge from deciding in their favour—if they'd been cut out entirely, they might have been able to persuade someone they had a case. But he's been generous enough to show any court that they're just money-grabbers trying for all they can get—"

Ralphie had raised his head, not quite turning to her, but seemed to be following some train of thought. Wavering, perhaps, in the unquestioning loyalty his mother demanded.

"I don't—" She raised her voice, pitching it across the room so that they could all hear. So that Ralphie could hear and know her good intentions. "I don't want the money!"

It silenced the room. Heads turned towards her again, hope and satisfaction mingling on faces.

"That isn't legal," the lawyer disclaimed hastily. "It doesn't mean a thing. You can't hold her to it. As her legal adviser, I must point out—"

"I don't—" She could feel hysteria rising within her. "I don't want the money!"

At last, Ralphie moved.

"Don't be too hasty, dearest." He was at her side. "Mr. Clements is right. We must think this over carefully."

Behind him, the relatives shifted, parted and re-grouped, forming new battle lines. Now Ralphie's mother was left standing alone, considering—calculating—the import of what she had just heard.

So much for all the secrecy. So much for "breaking it gently to Mother."

"I'm afraid we've been keeping it 'our little secret,'" Ralphie smirked across the room at his mother. "With the Old Man so sick, it didn't seem the time to announce it. But, well, the fact is—Val and I are going to be married."

It was the way he said it, the faint flourish of cupidity, of self-congratulation, in his tone that told Val the truth. He had never intended to marry her. Not until this moment. That had been the real reason for all the secrecy. He had thought he'd been on to a good thing, that was all. He'd been getting everything he wanted, giving nothing in return, intending to give nothing in return. Letting her believe what she wanted to, perhaps laughing at her naïveté. How could she have imagined that he—with his famous background, his famous breeding—would bother to marry a penniless little English nurse? She was fun to sleep with, that was all. When the time came to marry, he had intended to look around for some girl in his own social class—preferably an heiress in her own right.

Was that what Horatio had been trying to convey to her? Was that why he had left her the money? As a lever, so that she could get what she really wanted—if, after having discovered the truth, it was still what she wanted?

She stepped back half a pace, unnoticed, and studied Ralphie carefully. Did she really want to buy him? Would he be, after all, such a good bargain?

"My dears—" His mother came forward, purring, her choice made. Not that there had been any real choice about

it. Not to have to share the fortune with all the other relatives, but to acquire sole—or almost sole—rights to it
through her son's marriage.

"My dears—" Her words embraced both of them, but
her approving eyes were on Ralphie. "How clever of you."

Then the rest of the family began moving towards them
cautiously. Perhaps, after all, it might not be so bad. If the
money were not actually going out of the family. Or, rather,
were being brought back into the family almost immediately by the brilliant fast-thinking and noble self-sacrifice
of Clever Ralphie.

The murmurs of congratulation began to grow. Behind
the bland smiles, the calculation grew. How would it affect
each one of them personally? They paid lip service to Val,
but their real attention was centred on Ralphie's mother. As
though Val herself were negligible. As though Ralphie's
mother would be in control of the fortune.

Certainly, Ralphie would never dispute his mother's
right to do as she wished with the money. Ralphie would
always take his mother's side in any argument. Somehow,
she had always known that—it had been one of the
thoughts she had pushed aside, trying to insist to herself
that love could conquer all. Ralphie would not consider his
wife to have any say in the matter. Once they were married,
he would believe that the money was his own. He could
justify such an attitude so conveniently—it was family
money, it should never have been willed away from the family. In this town, such an attitude would not need justification.

"A simple ceremony, I think—" Already Ralphie's
mother had taken over, was making all the plans. "Later
we'll have a formal reception for our friends, all that. But,
right now—" She dabbed at her eyes with the scrap of lace
she had been viciously twisting earlier, as though belatedly
remembering that the day had started with the Old Man's
funeral.

"Everyone will understand," she said firmly, her tone
daring anyone not to. "It's only natural that we won't want a

sad—but inevitable—occasion to stand in the way of the happiness of our young ones."

Val had turned and met the lawyer's eyes. Those sad, cynical, quizzical eyes. Eyes that had seen it all and were watching it through for yet another time. Eyes that recognized what was happening—and wondered whether she did.

Val did. She was being rushed into something irrevocable. ("One thing I can't stand is being hustled . . ." the Old Man's voice came back to her. "And this family will do it every time—if you let them.")

Val smiled faintly at the lawyer and saw his face relax, one corner of his mouth twitch. He knew—or suspected now—what was going to happen. Furthermore, he approved. He could not have been the Old Man's friend and crony if he did not.

She should have known, she told herself grimly. If she hadn't been so caught up with Horatio, fighting his last battle with him, perhaps she might have paid more attention to the warning signals. For one thing, she might have spared a moment to realize that—despite the ridiculous American affinity for diminutives—there was something wrong with a man going into his thirties who was content to allow himself to be called "Ralphie."

Oh yes, he was his mother's boy, all right. As he could never be his wife's.

Even now the hand that rested on Ralphie's sleeve curled around his arm like a predatory claw. She turned, and her other grasping claw reached out for Val.

"My dears, I think, in honour of the occasion, we might break out some champagne. It isn't every day that my son announces his engagement."

"No!" Val said. Automatically, she had shied back from that hand, then found that she was repelled by the whole idea.

"Come, dear, don't be shy—" Ralphie's mother seemed suddenly to realize that her prospective daughter-in-law had not rushed forward gratefully to be embraced.

"Come on, sweetheart." Ralphie turned to her, his smile masking a faint impatience. *Everyone* ought to jump when *Mother* spoke. "This is our engagement party."

"No." She took another step backwards and found Lawyer Clements's arm around her waist, supporting her, encouraging her. "No, it isn't."

"Oh, now, look." His forehead wrinkled faintly while he stretched his mouth a bit wider. "Just because the day started on a sombre note—" surely an understatement to describe the Grand Old Man's funeral, she though wildly—"that doesn't mean it has to end on one. Let's cheer up. We're going to be married—let's tell the world and celebrate."

"No," she said. "No, we're not."

"What?" The smile disappeared, the frown came into its own. "You're upset. You don't know what you're saying." How could any woman refuse *him*? The smile crept back—understanding, forgiving.

"It's the excitement. The strain. It's all been too much for you. We'll just have a glass of champagne and then—"

"No," she repeated, with finality. "I'm not going to marry you."

The relatives drew back once more. Ralphie's mother dropped the pseudo-welcoming hand. In some way, by rejecting Ralphie, she was rejecting all of them. Furthermore, they divined—rightly—that she did not now intend to reject the money. The atmosphere chilled noticeably.

"The little slut—" One of the relatives spoke for all of them. "Killing's too good for her!" . . .

"You all right?" The salesgirl yanked the curtain aside, squinting in at her.

"Oh, er, yes." How long had she been standing here, lost in memories of the past? The recent past, but past, nonetheless.

"That is—the zipper—" she fabricated quickly. "I—I can't seem to—It seems to be jammed—"

Expertly, the salesgirl spun her round and tugged at the zipper. She gave no indication of surprise when it yielded instantly. Customers were like that. "It's all right now."

"Oh, thank you." Val stepped out of the dress. "I—I'll have this one. And the grey. But not the other—it doesn't suit me."

The salesgirl nodded, swept up the two indicated garments, and moved off, shutting the curtains behind her.

Slowly, Val got back into her uniform, armouring herself for the last time in its starched white anonymity. Tonight she would keep her promise to Mrs. Abercrombie and pack the uniform away for the remainder of their association. Perhaps for the remainder of her life. Certainly, she need never earn her living by nursing again . . .

The trial by media had been more painful and harder to endure than the actual court case. The newspaper headlines, the lurking television cameras, the reporters dogging her steps, all inflamed by the reckless charges issued by Ralphie and the relatives, and protected from the libel laws by the ability to attribute these statements as direct quotes by the relatives concerned.

"Undue Influence" . . . and all that that implied when an elderly male patient and a pretty young female nurse were involved. Even now, thinking of it, she still felt besmirched.

She had won the case—as Lawyer Clements had foretold—but lost her reputation. Fortunately, after a coast-to-coast start, the discovery of a local New York scandal and an international air disaster had reduced the court proceedings to a matter of interest only in the State itself and the nearest surrounding States. But that had been publicity enough. Too much.

It was not surprising that the media found her guilty. It was to the credit of American justice—and Lawyer Clements—that the court had upheld the Will.

Walking down the courthouse steps, with the spectators booing and the occasional gob of spittle landing at her feet, she had halted abruptly when confronted by Ralphie.

Ralphie with the gloves off, his face contorted, damply vicious, had snarled, "You won't get away with this!"

"We intend to appeal." Immediately behind him, his mother quickly softened what had sounded like a physical threat, even to the surrounding spectators sympathetic to their cause. "We will take our appeal to the highest authority in the land. To the Supreme Court—if necessary."

"Take it where you like." Lawyer Clements must have been well instructed, and well paid, by the Old Man. Or perhaps he had a few scores of his own to settle with the family. "You'll still lose." His hand at Val's elbow, he continued to urge her forward down the steps.

"I swear to you—" Ralphie retreated before them, still shaking with rage—"I'll pay you back somehow. You won't get away with this!"

And, in the background, someone behind him murmured again, "Killing's too good for her!" . . .

"No reason for you to hang around waiting for the Appeal to be heard," Lawyer Clements had said comfortingly to her later. "These things take a long time—even though the other party hasn't a leg to stand on. You needn't even be here when it's heard. I'll take care of everything. In fact, you're looking far too peaked, you ought to get away for a bit—it would help put everything into perspective."

"Perhaps you're right," Val said. Suddenly, the thought of going back to work shimmered enticingly before her, promising a haven from her own problems, the opportunity of doing something useful again.

"You needn't worry about money," he said. "You can take all you want from the drawing account. It was part of the arrangements made at the same time Horatio made his Will. There'll be no problem about it. Why don't you go down to Florida—get a bit of sunshine—?"

"Yes, fine," she said vaguely, feeling that it might be better if he didn't know too much about her plans. If no one knew too much about her plans . . .

Chapter 14

"I want a nice present for a lady." The voice, determined and slightly defiant, made Gloria look up from the negotiations with the manageress which were, in any case, almost completed now. This was a familiar situation to her: the male at bay in a ladies' gift shop, not sure what he wanted, but ready to pay plenty for it, equating expense with taste. The test of a good salesgirl was the way she coped.

But this salesgirl already had a customer. A good one, to judge from the way she began making out a sales slip for two dresses rather than one. It did not justify, however, her ignoring the prospective customer in front of her.

The manageress gave a short explosive sound and moved forward quickly. "A present for a lady?" she said. "Of course. What did you have in mind?"

"Something nice," the customer said. They always did—as though you might think they wanted to buy something nasty.

Gloria was drawn automatically into the orbit of the sale, unable to resist a demonstration of someone else's technique. These people were going to be handling the Gloria Grandi line on all future voyages; she wanted to make absolutely certain they knew what they were doing.

The customer turned slightly and she recognized Dick Slade. But he was a widower. A present for a lady? He had been very attentive to the woman in the wheelchair lately—and she was most definitely a lady. Was this to be a farewell present—or just an au revoir? There was something in the air between them, that much was certain. People were beginning to notice it. Too bad he hadn't had longer to make his pitch. Still, he could undoubtedly manage to run into her again once they were ashore. Tourist Europe wasn't all that big.

There was something else about this guy, though . . . something she ought to remember. Something that might be useful, that had promised to tie in with another idea she had had. Gloria wrinkled her forehead briefly, and then she had it.

Toys. He was a toy manufacturer. Well, retired now, but he might still have some contacts—was almost bound to have. You don't build up a business and spend your life in that business without knowing all about your business friends and rivals. Yes, retired or not, Dick Slade could be very useful to her right now.

Gloria bent over and scooped up Guido's leading reins. She straightened and tugged at them gently, hoping he would take the hint and come upright of his own accord. Sometimes he did, and sometimes he didn't. But it was awkward for her to have to get down and lift him, and she didn't want to appear awkward in front of Dick Slade. A little more insistently, she tugged at the reins again.

Guido lurched to his feet and stood there, swaying unsteadily. From somewhere down below there came a long high-pitched metallic grating sound, as though a giant iron fingernail had been pulled at an angle across a smooth steel slate. The ship gave a convulsive shudder at the same time.

The *Beatrice Cenci* wasn't the only one to shudder at the noise. Gloria's spine stiffened in involuntary protest, the manageress and salesgirl murmured something violent-sounding in a native argot new to Gloria. Even Dick Slade looked upset.

Guido flung his hands over his ears, tangling nougat in the baby silk strands of his hair, and tottered to bury his head at a point where her lap might have been had she been sitting down.

The skirt was ancient, Gloria reminded herself grimly, its indeterminate length already a damning admission of its age, and she had said good-bye to those tights the first night aboard when they had snagged on some unnoticed flaw in a chair in her cabin. Nevertheless, her inner being quailed at the thought of good material being subjected to the sticky onslaught.

"It's all right, baby." She eased Guido away from her. "It's only the funny boat. Ha-ha? Ha-ha?" she coaxed pleadingly.

"Ha-ha," Guido responded obligingly, if a trifle uncertainly. He pushed himself into an independent stance, swaggering a trifle, like his father, and rammed the remaining lump of nougat into his mouth again. "Ha-ha."

"Good little kid—" Dick Slade glanced down at Guido, sparing a moment from the lavish array of possible gifts the manageress was spreading before him. "He's got guts. I like that in a kid. He'll go far."

"Sure, he will." Gloria smiled back, taking instant advantage of the opening. "He's already my market research expert, isn't he?"

"Is he?" Caught, as she had hoped he would be, the ex-manufacturer stared down at Guido. "How does he do that?"

"Very charming, signor. *Très gentil*—" The manageress tried to recapture his attention, shaking out a cashmere stole, delicate as a spider's web, soft as a cloud, for his approval.

"Yuh. Nice, very nice." His glance was perfunctory, his real attention still held by Gloria and Guido.

"I'm thinking of putting in a new line. I'm the Gloria Grandi Shoppes—" She paused expectantly, but his nod was perfunctory and purely political, she could tell. Well, why should he have heard of her? She might be a New York institution, but that didn't mean the rest of the country had to know her. It took more than the occasional ad in the *New Yorker* to make yourself a household name.

And perhaps it had been a bit overdone to say "Shoppes" like that—as though there were a whole string of them. But the manageress was listening with more avidity than appeared on the surface and she wanted her to keep thinking she was on to a good thing in being allowed to handle Gloria Grandi goods.

Guido was obviously beginning to feel neglected. He began to waver towards Dick Slade, but Gloria pulled on the reins, checking him firmly. Just because a man had manufactured toys, it didn't necessarily follow that he liked kids. Anyway, nobody was very fond of having sticky fingers plastered all over a clean suit. Until she could get him back to the cabin and thoroughly washed, Guido was persona non grata.

"Fine, I'll take that." Dick Slade's attention had gone back to the cashmere stole. He pulled out a bulging wallet and counted out some bills. Strange how many men still preferred to take the risk of losing cash rather than buy travellers' cheques. Or perhaps, Gloria thought, he had an even bigger wallet of cheques tucked away somewhere for shore use.

"Gift wrap it, will you?" He gave the manageress a fatuous grin. "It's for a very special lady."

The curtain to the fitting-room rattled back and Gloria glanced instinctively in that direction. So, it was the little nurse, was it, who was buying two dresses in this exclusive shop? Some people got very nice tips at the end of a case.

Val hesitated in the opening, as though she would retreat at the sight of Dick Slade, then came forward resolutely, a thin smile on her face. *She*, now, had a very impressive pad of travellers' cheques. So, not a tip—perhaps some money in her own right. Or perhaps, Gloria toyed with the idea of scandal, she had been entrusted with the purse-keeping for the trip and was treating herself to a few little perks along the way.

The thought immediately made Gloria uncomfortable, bringing as it did in its immediate train, an instant apprehension as to what Lorenzo might be getting up to in the Shoppe without her.

Shoppe—Shoppes. Their most recent, and torrid, quarrel came back to haunt her. Something else she had Joe to thank for. Good old helpful Joe, who had found such a good buy out on Long Island. In one of the best resorts. A summer shop with living accommodation included. And then taken such pains to persuade Lorenzo that it was every

American child's birthright: the summer cottage in a fashionable resort. With the fact of a shop attached making it a wonderful business proposition—so good that even a woman ought to be able to recognize it, to want to take advantage of it.

First, consolidate the advantages you've gained. It was a principle of business she could not make Lorenzo understand. He considered her refusal to be some obscure form of miserliness—possibly, even, of pique, because he had been the one to discover this unique opportunity.

Useless to try to explain to him that the overheads connected with another shop would preclude the capital outlay necessary to acquire the Long Island property. And the mortgage he was suggesting, again prompted by Joe, would mean back-breaking repayments which might not be justified by the returns from the shop over the first few years while it was getting started. Especially as it would only be in operation for six to eight months of the year.

"It will be a good place for Guido," Lorenzo had maintained stubbornly. "The sun, the sand, the sea. Not the hot New York in the summer."

"Listen, Guido's just a baby," Gloria had argued reasonably. "In a few years, sure, maybe. Fine. Right now, for Christ's sake, he doesn't know whether it's New York City or Wednesday."

"A lady does not swear." Lorenzo's face was shuttered again, implacable.

"No—you're damned right she doesn't. And that kind of a lady never makes any money, either!"

Oh, Joe would have been proud of himself if he could have heard the fight that went on after that. Or maybe he did. Maybe he got a blow-by-blow account from Lorenzo. Or maybe not. Lorenzo would not want to admit that she had thrown her earning capacity in his face—and at the same time as vetoing one of his own money-making schemes.

It wasn't easy, being the one with the money. The hardest part was trying *not* to slam it at him when they had a fight. So far, she had managed to hold back the really

unforgivable question: *Would you have married me if I
hadn't had money?*

Dick Slade was leaving the shop. Lost in her thoughts,
Gloria had nearly lost him. Tugging at Guido's reins, she
hurried after Dick Slade. It was just about now or never.
That was the trouble with ocean travel, you were just getting to know people when the voyage ended. Still, it was
better than air travel—when you scarcely had time to strike
up a conversation at all.

"Toys!" she gasped, coming up behind Dick Slade.

"What?" He jumped as though he had been shot,
whirling around to face her.

"I mean—that's what Guido is going to advise me on."
He must think her demented. Certainly, he looked as
though he were going to start backing away. "I mean, you
asked what he did. But then you started buying the cashmere—"

"Oh, I see." He still sounded faintly mollifying, as
though he were humouring her. "Yes, yes. That's very good.
Ha-ha." His eyes twitched beyond her, seeking escape.

"I thought toys would be a good addition to the Gloria
Grandi line. Not just any old toys, but a selective—"

"I'm sure you're right." He tried to sidestep her, but
Guido had strayed to the other side of the companionway
and his leash stretched across the passage. Dick Slade
would have to leap over it like a jumping rope if he wanted
to get away in that direction. He took a firmer grip on his
gift-wrapped package and looked as though he might be
considering it.

"I thought—" Gloria moved to block him. "I mean, I
hope I don't sound too presumptuous, but I thought perhaps you might be willing to help me a little."

"Sure. I will if I can." His eyes did not quite match the
calm assurance of his tone, they were still shifting restlessly,
looking for a way out. "What can I do?"

"Well, I thought—you having been in the manufacturing end of the toy business—"

"I'm retired now," he said quickly. "I sold out my share

of the business. I haven't had anything to do with it for two or three years now."

"But you still must know lots of people," Gloria persisted. "People still in the business—maybe your old factory even. I mean, if they're doing any really new lines that might go—"

"Yes, I see." He nodded briskly, still not looking very pleased about it. Probably she shouldn't have blurted it out like that. She should have led up to it more subtly, but she'd thought he was going to get away and she'd really wanted to know.

"Yes, I ought to be able to do something for you." He gave her a mechanical smile. "I don't have my address book on me at the moment, of course—"

"Oh, I didn't mean right this instant." Surely, she hadn't sounded that bad. "I mean, if you could write to me later—" She fumbled for her business card. "And perhaps you could write or telephone your friends and let them know I'll be contacting them."

"I'll be glad to do that." He chuckled with genuine amusement, something seemed to have restored his good humour. Of course, it was an awfully cute little business card—one of her artist friends had designed it.

"I'd be very grateful," she said earnestly. "And if you'd like to drop in at the shop any time, I'd be very pleased to allow you a trade discount on anything you might like to buy. Who knows—" she smiled at him archly— "you might be looking for another present for a lady."

"In Parliament this afternoon, in reply to a question from the House, the Prime Minister said that—"

Susan replaced the receiver. That was where she had come in. No real news anywhere.

The telephone rang almost immediately. She picked it up with a faint feeling of surprise, almost of guilt, as though the Prime Minister might have rung back annoyed at being cut off in the midst of one of his pronouncements.

"You didn't come up on deck this afternoon," the voice accused as soon as she had said hello.

145

"Oh, Ben. No, I didn't. I wasn't feeling well." She hesitated, then lied deliberately, it was the easiest way out. "My leg was bothering me."

"Oh." That had stopped him cold. It always did. Either they tried to pretend there was nothing the matter with her at all, or they treated her like a cripple. Either way, they hated to have her make reference to her condition.

"You're better now," he said, so flatly it was as much a statement as a question.

"Yes," she said.

"You'll be at the Gala Dinner tonight?"

"Yes."

"I'll see you in the dining salon, then. Perhaps we might go for a stroll on deck afterwards. I understand we're due to pass a sister ship about ten—it ought to be something to see."

"Yes," she said, "I'd like that." It would add a festive note to the trip—and heaven knew the trip could stand one.

"Good," he said. "We've got ourselves a date. I'll look forward to it."

"So will I," she said, and could not tell whether he had already hung up or not.

She replaced her own receiver slowly, thinking. She liked Ben as well as she liked anybody on board—perhaps more. He knew nothing of her past or her future, yet he kept seeking her out. They shared only the present, and that was growing shorter by the moment.

If she were sensible—It was something she had faced in New York—rather, not faced. Just taken one quick horrified look and turned away. But the fact remained. If she were sensible, she would make her own Will. Right now. Before going ashore. Before meeting Eric again.

She had quite a lot to leave. Rather, in another two weeks, she would have a lot to leave. She could not die intestate and risk Eric profiting from any part of it. Therefore, the sensible thing to do was to leave it to someone else—to anyone else.

To someone who had no interest in it—who did not

know it existed and thus could not complain when she made a later Will assigning it elsewhere. As, eventually, she would undoubtedly wish to do.

Professor Benjamin Cook fitted the bill—rather, the Will—perfectly.

Perhaps she was just being paranoiac about the whole thing. Perhaps Eric had settled down to the life of a gentleman farmer and harboured no thought of harming her. It was possible that he did not even remember the incident that had marked her so permanently—people had a great faculty for forgetting anything discreditable to themselves. Perhaps he could now watch her limp across a room with no more than a faint sympathy, his conscious mind having blotted out all knowledge that he was in any way to blame. Perhaps.

The sight of his face when she told him that she had already made a Will ensuring that nothing would ever come to him if anything should happen to her might tell her more about his memory—and his future plans.

Which was why it was so important that she should leave everything to someone who knew nothing of her circumstances. Then, if by any chance Eric got to her before he could learn that it wasn't any use, the legatee could stand up to any amount of police investigation and eventually inherit.

And who better than Professor Benjamin Cook? A respectable teacher on a well-earned sabbatical leave should stand up to any amount of investigation. He would be amazed, of course, and eventually delighted with his luck. The money would be a godsend to him and he could sell up and stud farm and the estate if he wished. He would have enough to devote the rest of his life to his research and writing instead of a single sabbatical year.

She smiled. It would be ironic if, out of the warfare between them, she and Eric contributed some works of lasting scholarship to posterity.

She sat down at the writing desk and pulled out a sheet of notepaper. A holograph Will was as binding as any that a solicitor could produce with parchment and seals. Just keep it simple—that was the cardinal rule. That—and the one about two independent witnesses.

Beneath the engraving of the *Beatrice Cenci* with all flags flying, she began to write. "I, SUSAN MARGOT EMERY . . ."

When it was finished she rang for the steward and the stewardess. Only the stewardess answered her bell.

"No," Susan said. "I want the steward, too."

"He is busy," the stewardess said. "He will come later."

"No—" Susan remembered that much. "Get someone else then. I require two of you, here together at the same time. I want you to witness my signature."

The stewardess shrugged and went out. When she returned shortly, she had one of the ship's officers in tow. He was, Susan recalled vaguely, the one called Angelo.

"Good." She smiled briefly at them. "I want you to watch me sign this. It is my Will—"

Angelo made a protesting movement.

"That's all right," Susan said, before he could launch into any flowery protestations about her youth and health, if not her beauty. The beautiful died, too. "It's just a precaution."

"Ah, si," he said. "I understand."

For an odd moment, she had the feeling that he really did.

Chapter 15

There were the bottles of champagne from Mildred and Augustus, plus the complimentary wine from the *Beatrice Cenci*, to keep the party merry. The waiters didn't bother waiting for orders since the Gala Dinner was, traditionally, the one meal of the voyage when the passengers ate their way through every course on the menu. The only question was whether they wished steak or turkey for the main course.

During the progress of the festive meal, from somewhere beneath their feet, the long agonized metallic screech came again, momentarily silencing the salon. Then someone whooped out, "Now, that's what *I* call a groaning board!" Someone else countered, "Sounds more like indigestion to me!" And they all laughed uproariously.

None of them noticed the waiters' quick roll of the eyes to heaven. Nor the surreptitious glancing at watches while strained smiles masked the calculations: How close to port? How many more hours to go until safely within sight of land? Within the reach of help from shore?

Don't alarm the passengers—one of the unwritten laws of the sea.

And so, the waiters rushed to refill glasses at tables where the merriment flagged. To readjust a paper hat to a more ludicrous angle, to pause and clown reassuringly with a bottle, a balloon, a streamer, a handful of confetti—with anything that would make the passengers laugh and divert their attention from what might be happening below.

Until, finally . . . the coffee and Strega. The autographing of menus . . . the last cigar and cigarette . . . the exchanging of addresses . . . the promises to meet again

. . . to keep in touch . . . the concerned little huddles, with whispers which broke off as a waiter approached, "How much are *you* tipping tomorrow?" . . .

Finally, the passengers departed, the dining salon was cleared, the crew were free to drop their masks . . . and worry.

Moving quickly from his own table, Dick Slade appropriated Mrs. Abercrombie's wheelchair before Val could register any sort of protest—if, indeed, Mrs. Abercrombie had not flashed her a signal denying her right to make any objections. There was a quick glimpse of a gaily-wrapped package dropped into Mrs. Abercrombie's lap, a glint of light along the metal of the wheelchair—and then a curious emptiness as they departed swiftly. As though, Val thought dismally, her very reason for existing had suddenly been snatched away from her.

Val stood up, trying not to notice that most of the others were pairing off. She walked out of the dining salon smoothly and firmly, not looking back lest she should see someone notice that she was alone. She didn't want anyone to feel sorry for her, to call her back and annex her as part of an unwilling threesome. She had had her share of pairing off, what she needed now was time to recover and rediscover herself again.

"You do not go up on deck?" Angelo was standing in front of her as she turned down the passageway to her cabin.

"I'm tired," she said. "And I still have some packing to do for Mrs. Abercrombie."

"Packing!" He shrugged. "You have plenty of time tomorrow for packing. All day."

"We *are* going to make port tomorrow?" Val was instantly suspicious. There had been too many rumours of delays.

Again the shrug, a spread of the hands to consign shipping schedules into the care of the Deity. From below, distant and echoing at this point, a muffled metallic groan. Angelo winced slightly.

"It is better we do not try to go too fast," he said.

"What *is* that?"

"Is nothing." He smiled blandly. "Come up on deck for a little while. You will see a sight you don't forget. Very soon now, we pass our sister ship, the *Eleanora Duse,* and we salute each other. The whistles blow, the bells ring, all the passengers cheer and wave. It is very exciting, very gay—so much noise you can't hear yourself scream."

He seemed to think that was a recommendation. Val smiled faintly. Perhaps it would be rather fun, something to talk about later, to remember about the voyage.

"All right," she said. "I'll come on deck long enough to see the ships pass in the night."

Guido was nearly asleep when the knock came at the door. He bounced back to wakefulness and struggled upright. "Da-da?" he suggested hopefully.

"No," Gloria pushed him back gently. "Daddy is at home in New York—I've told you that. We're on board a ship. We're going to see your great-grandad now. We won't see Daddy again until we get home."

The knock came again. Guido squirmed away from her restraining hand and stared bright-eyed at the door.

"All right," Gloria said. "I'll show you. But stay there. Don't get up."

She swung the door open and stepped back in surprise. She had expected to find the stewardess there. "Oh!—Good evening, Father—"

"Good evening." He stepped into the cabin as though he had been invited to and closed the door behind him. Gloria stood staring.

"Da-da?" Guido was staring, too. "Da-da?" he queried uncertainly.

"Not quite." The man smiled at Guido briefly and turned to Gloria. "There's something I feel I should explain," he said. "I understand you've been asking questions—"

"Oh, no!" She felt guilty colour flooding her face. "It wasn't like that—I only thought—" She broke off, to voice what she had thought would only make the situation worse. There were so many wavering priests now, so many vows broken or challenged, so many suspicions one might have that the field was wide open for any supposition.

"Yes," he said wryly. "That's what I thought you might be thinking. That's why I wanted to explain—" He glanced uneasily at Guido. "Can you come up on deck for a little while? I won't keep you long."

"Well, I was planning to have an early night—"

"I won't keep you long," he said again. "In any case, you wouldn't be able to sleep. We're passing another ship of the line any time now. You know what that means. Whistles, bells, noise enough to wake the dead—"

"I heard something about it," Gloria said. "I hadn't realized it was this soon."

"You won't be able to sleep anyway," he said. "You might as well come up on deck and join the party."

"Yes . . ." Gloria said doubtfully. He looked strange tonight. Different. For one thing, he wasn't wearing his Roman collar. He was in a dark shirt and slacks, with a dark jacket. The thought came to her that he would be lost among the dark shadows on deck. It would be like talking to a shadow to have a conversation with him.

"Get your coat," he prodded. "Hurry up—if you don't want to miss all the excitement."

"All right." She came to a decision. "We'll be right with you."

"We?" He looked thoroughly disconcerted.

"Naturally." Gloria glanced at him curiously, gathering up the baby's clothes. "You didn't think I'd leave Guido here alone, did you?"

"Er . . . ah . . . no." He still seemed taken aback. "I . . . er . . . thought you might call the stewardess in to sit with him. We won't be long."

"Leave him with a stranger? With all that noise going on all over the ship? He'd be frightened." It was easy to tell the good Father wasn't accustomed to children and their ways. Nor, for that matter, to mothers.

"Here we go, baby." Guido bounced up to meet her half-way, gurgling with glee as she reclothed him.

"But . . . er . . ."

"As long as he's with me, he'll be all right." She did not add that she would be glad to have the dubious chaperonage that Guido would provide. For some reason, Father Service was making her feel extremely uncomfortable tonight.

"Yes, of course." Helplessly, he watched her fasten the bright red harness straps around the chunky little chest.

"He can see for himself what all the excitement is about and he won't be frightened." She snapped the reins to the harness and looked about for her own coat.

"Yes, I see." Abstractedly, he collected her coat from across the chair where she had tossed it when she came in from being on deck that afternoon and held it for her. "But—"

"He'll enjoy it." Firmly, she cut off any further protests he might be going to make. Guido was already half-way across the room to the door. "You see, he can't wait to get up there."

"Yes, he's very enthusiastic."

Which was more than could be said for Father Service. He looked as though he now wished he had never thought of the whole idea. Or perhaps what he had wanted to say no longer seemed so important to him.

"Come on—" Gloria swooped and snatched up the end of Guido's reins, laughing with him as he reached eagerly for the doorknob. "Let's go see another pretty ship."

"There she is," Ben Cook said. "Over on the horizon—just coming into view."

"Where?" Susan tried to follow his pointing finger. "I don't—Oh yes, I do." A clustered sparkle of lights shone against the horizon and advanced in stately progress. "She doesn't seem to be coming very fast."

"I don't suppose she is," he laughed. "Poor *Eleanora Duse*—I'm afraid her nose is badly out of joint. *She* was the flagship of the line before the *Beatrice Cenci* was commissioned."

"So, you mean even though they're sister ships, they're rivals?"

"Sisters often are."

Already passengers were crowding the rails, pointing to the approaching liner. The babble of voices grew; someone started a premature cheer.

"Let's walk on the other side for a while." Ben Cook grimaced distastefully at his fellow-passengers. "It will be quieter. We can come back when the ships pass. There's still plenty of time."

He took Susan's arm and steered her gently through a party of passengers who had obviously bluffed their way up from Tourist quarters, having equally obviously taken full advantage of the free wine at dinner. On the last night out, such things were shrugged at by crew members whose attention was already focused on the more serious problems of disembarkation tomorrow and the need to collect and make ready the piles of luggage already being set outside cabin doors.

The other side of the deck might have been on a different ship, it was so deserted. Fog had returned with the night and seemed thicker here, blurring the overhead lights and making unexpected pools of darkness at the far end of the deck where the railing could not be seen.

The motion of the sea was more noticeable here. It was not so calm as she had thought, the press of people and the cheerful hubbub had been distracting enough to mask the fact that it was still fairly rough. Not nearly so rough as it had been in mid-ocean, but rough enough to remind one that storms were still raging over the waves behind them, stirring up a deep swell. The deck rolled steeply beneath their feet as if in reminder that they were still a long way from harbour.

They walked in companionable silence, passing a few other couples who had strayed from the livelier side of the ship. But a few steps put enough fog between them and the others to make it seem as though they had the deck to themselves.

"Damn!" Ben shuddered as the agonized metallic groan—now become as omnipresent and persistent as the foghorn had been earlier—sounded again from somewhere in the depths of the cargo hold. "I hate that noise! Wouldn't you think they'd have done something about it by now?"

"It probably isn't worth their bothering about," Susan soothed. She smiled and nodded to Gloria and little Guido as they passed, feeling a faint surprise that the cleric with them seemed to be looking so intently, almost angrily, down at Guido. "We'll be in port tomorrow and they can fix whatever it is much more easily then."

"I suppose you're right, but—" He shrugged uneasily. "I still don't like it."

They were rounding the stern of the vessel now, the patchy mist thinner here, they could see the broad white wake spreading out behind the *Beatrice Cenci* charting her passage. The lights of the *Eleanora Duse* were considerably closer now. As many passengers were crowding the port side railing as would be there straining for first sight of relatives when they gained harbour tomorrow. Susan wondered vaguely if there was anyone at all attending the film show tonight.

Even as she recognized Val and Angelo, they broke away from the crowd at the railing and began a promenade towards the deserted side of the ship. They were talking earnestly and did not appear to notice anyone else. She noticed with approval that Val no longer wore her uniform. Without it, she looked younger, prettier—and more vulnerable. Little wonder that an enterprising ship's officer might try to snatch a last-minute shipboard romance with such an attractive girl.

"Wait a minute—" The increased pressure on her arm halted her as she tried to turn to walk up the crowded, brightly-lit deck. "I want—"

"But we'll be passing any moment now," she protested. "I don't want to miss it."

"No." He cast an appraising eye at the distance still separating the sister ships. "We've got a few minutes yet. Time for one more turn up and down the deck."

"But—" Susan tried to pull away, suddenly reluctant to be alone with him any longer. He was too intense, abruptly more of a stranger than he had seemed for some time.

"No," he repeated. The *Beatrice Cenci* bucked unexpectedly beneath their feet, riding a wave higher than the others. "No." His vice-like grip tightened inexorably around her arm, drawing her back into the emptiness, the darkness.

"We still have things to say to each other."

"Almost time for the excitement to begin," Butler said genially.

"I don't want to miss it." She had said that before.

"Don't worry," he said. "I'll get you back there in time. You won't miss any of the excitement."

"Then you'd better hurry." But a lilt of laughter in her voice softened the semi-order.

"Don't worry, sweetheart. I'll make sure you get the best view on the ship." And the best view off the ship—a water-line view. Not many people ever saw a ship from that angle.

"If you're sure—" She turned awkwardly to look up at him, but he was looking out to sea, keeping an eye on the *Eleanora Duse*, and that seemed to reassure her.

They might all get a closer view of the *Eleanora Duse* than they had anticipated. Butler watched her approach with a growing uneasiness. She appeared to have speeded up and to be moving towards them on a collision course—as though she were going to ram them broadside.

Of course, it was just an illusion, a trick of perspective. It might even be a trick cooked up by the captains of both ships to give the passengers a thrill. A grandstand play, making it look as though they were going to come dangerously close, then veering off at the last minute. Relief would make the cheers twice as loud when the ships passed safely.

Except that the *Beatrice Cenci* didn't seem to be co-operating fully in the game. She was not hurrying full speed ahead to the rendezvous with her sister ship. Instead she dipped into every wave trough and quivered there momentarily, dragging her heels while the deep protesting moan was torn from her anew.

Butler frowned. Was that inner groan getting louder? With all the noise coming from the passengers, he couldn't be sure. He wished that they would all shut up. Not shut up permanently—he needed the covering noise in case she screamed—but shut up just long enough to let him take a good listen and try to figure out what was happening down below.

Not that it mattered. Butler glanced at a passing crew member who seemed unconcerned. If anything were really wrong, the crew ought to be looking a lot more worried.

Butler grinned quietly. In a few minutes, the crew were going to have plenty to worry about.

Not much longer now. Up to the front of the ship, then—on the way back—when all the attention was concentrated on passing the *Eleanora Duse*—

Carefully, almost tenderly, he steered his highly-valued companion towards the prow of the ship, bending solicitously to catch some comment she was making.

Vaguely, he was aware of an occasional head turning as they passed, of the smile of approval from shipboard acquaintances still on this side of the ship. But they were thinning out now. One pair cut across them as they moved along, already crossing to the other side to watch the approaching *Eleanora Duse*.

"Shouldn't we get over there, too?" Once more she turned to look up at his face. "We'll miss everything."

"No, we won't." His smile was intended to be reassuring. Why, then, did she begin to look uneasy? Was there something in female intuition, after all? From the way most of his victims had behaved, he had always discounted it. But then he had never been quite so close to one of them before, nor for so long a time.

Imperceptibly, he speeded up their progress. Suddenly, he was irritable, keyed-up, anxious to get it over with. Nerves. They said an actor couldn't give a good performance unless he had opening-night nerves. His performances usually opened and closed the same night—no wonder his nerves responded so well.

But not this time. This time there was an additional problem. This time he couldn't melt away into the crowd and lose himself in the anonymous vastness of a large city. This time he had to stay on the scene until the ship docked. Moreover, some of the passengers had seen them together. It was unfortunate—but unavoidable. He would have to say that he had taken her back to her cabin—or left her on deck while he went to *his* cabin to get something he wanted to show her. Yes, that was better.

The starboard deck was deserted now; they had seen no one for the past few minutes. The crowd was all on the other side, the *Eleanora Duse*'s whistle had already begun some kind of preparatory throat-clearing. They should be at the passing point now.

But what was the matter with the *Beatrice Cenci*? As the *Eleanora Duse*'s speed had increased, hers had seemed to decrease. She had started out the voyage skimming over the waves like a seagull, now she was making heavy weather of every knot, like an old garbage scow that feared foundering with the next wave. And she hadn't been making that lousy noise when they sailed out of New York harbour, either. That dated from the night the storm was so bad. You couldn't tell him something hadn't happened then. He might not know anything about sailing, but he knew ships oughtn't to keep making a noise like that—

The noise came again, nearly drowned-out by the burgeoning cheers from passengers crowding the rails on both ships. Bells began ringing. The whistles of the *Eleanora Duse* and the *Beatrice Cenci* blasted deafeningly, excitedly, as though in parody of two long-lost travellers hailing each other in unexpected meeting.

"Let's get over there!" She twisted impatiently. "You said you'd get me over there in time to—"

"You're going over, all right, sweetheart." They were

practically lip-reading in the din. "You're going right over!" Relentlessly, he began pushing her towards the railing.

"What—?" She searched his face incredulously, finding neither mercy nor humanity there, only the grim intentness of his purpose, now unmistakable.

"Right over—" He mouthed at her. Something in her face, her expression, annoyed him. He didn't usually bother. But with this one, he decided to let her know what was happening to her—and why.

"Naughty Auntie," he said. "Taking too long to die. Mildred and Augustus got tired of waiting for their inheritance." They were nearly at the railing.

Mrs. Abercrombie stepped out of her wheelchair.

In an awkward sideways lurch, she was out and free of it. Her screams were lost in the bedlam from the other side of the ship.

Momentum carried Butler along for a couple more steps. A cold fury settled over him. Nobody had told him that the old bitch was able to walk. And nobody had told him that she wasn't. His anger was turning on himself now. He'd seen the wheelchair and assumed it. And assumptions were always dangerous.

He abandoned the empty wheelchair and dashed after Alicia Abercrombie. She hadn't got far and she had stopped screaming, probably realizing that it was useless and a waste of her fragile energy.

She faced him squarely as he came at her, having seen that the nearest doorway was too distant for her to make. At least she wasn't going to plead. It would have been no use, even if he could have heard above the din.

Her eyes moved beyond him, fixed on some point farther along the deck. But he knew there could be nothing down there but the empty wheelchair, rolling aimlessly in motion with the ship. "You don't get me to fall for that oldie, sweetheart. I don't turn around—you don't get away."

He snatched for her arm, but she was faster than he expected. He still kept the lingering remnants of that tattered idea that she was some kind of cripple. She evaded him.

The whistle of the *Beatrice Cenci* shrieked again in a wild elated frenzy. The *Eleanora Duse* answered with equally hysterical enthusiasm. The passengers whooped their own contribution to the pandemonium.

Through the windows of the deserted main lounge, Butler could see the *Eleanora Duse* sliding past majestically. Human marionettes lining her rails waved joyously to him, to anyone, trying to transmit their self-congratulation at being abroad on an adventure, heading for the New World, the streets paved with gold, the relatives who had struck it rich and were waiting for reinforcements to help with all the business.

Butler snarled wordlessly and lunged for Alice Abercrombie again. This was taking too long. Once the *Eleanora Duse* was passed, the passengers would begin straying all over the ship. It had to be accomplished *now*.

Mrs. Abercrombie had backed against the outer wall of the main lounge and was edging along it, as though she still hoped she might be able to reach the safety of a doorway. Her breath was coming in shallow gasps and her colour was bad. Throwing her overboard might be redundant, but he couldn't count on that. He was beginning to understand the annoyance Augustus had betrayed—she had as many lives as a cat.

The *Beatrice Cenci* gave a premonitory shudder. The agonized metallic groan was soundless in the rest of the uproar, but a deep warning vibrated upwards, striking through the decks and the soles of shoes, bringing uneasy frowns from passengers who did not even know why they should feel uneasy.

"Come on—" Butler captured her arm, dragging her towards the rail. "No good fighting it. You can't win—"

The wash from the *Eleanora Duse* hit the *Beatrice Cenci* like an overpowering personality swamping a lesser one. The *Beatrice Cenci* rolled desperately in the deep swell, weakened by her own lack of speed.

Butler staggered, trying to maintain his balance as the *Beatrice Cenci* surged upwards on the crest of the outermost wave of the backwash. The ships' whistles had stopped and the mood of the passengers was turning, their shrieks too high-pitched, their laughter faintly hysterical.

The *Beatrice Cenci* dropped sharply into the trough of the wave, throwing Butler and Mrs. Abercrombie back against a bulkhead. Butler lost his grip on her arm and she fell to her knees under the impact, but managed to claw a grip into the recessed ledge of one of the main lounge windows. Her other hand twined around the toggle bolt of the hatch that would secure the bulkhead if closed.

Butler swore as he saw the tenacity with which her fingers clung to their holds. From farther down the deck, he could hear a light persistent clatter—hadn't that damned wheelchair gone overboard yet?

"Come on—" Bracing his feet, he pulled at her shoulders, trying to tear her loose from her grip.

The *Beatrice Cenci* veered sharply in the other direction, throwing screaming passengers against the main lounge wall on the port side.

From below there came a final grinding shriek as the cargo shifted, the crates of heavy machinery breaking loose from their restraining chains, the automobiles hurtling forward to hammer against the hull of the ship.

The *Beatrice Cenci* heeled under the impact, fighting for her buoyancy, for her life, as the cargo tilted her over at a perilous angle. Engines skipped a beat, another beat, then throbbed strongly as they responded to new orders from the bridge. Like a wounded creature, the *Beatrice Cenci* lay sprawled atop the waves, seeming to hold her breath while the cargo rumbled and settled, until she knew that she would survive the night.

For Butler, it was too late. He had found himself clinging to Alicia Abercrombie for support as the ship threatened to capsize. She had tried feebly to shake him off without losing her own grip on safety.

Then something had slammed against the back of his knees, knocking his legs from under him. He had lost his hold on her as he fell and his fingers clawed uselessly at the smooth oily deckboards as he slid across the deck. He saw what had struck him—the wheelchair—still skittering

161

along the deck. Then he slid under the railing and could see nothing more.

His last thought as the icy paralysing waters closed over his head was that there were going to be a lot of dissatisfied ex-customers when his record file hit the Attorney General's desk.

Chapter 16

Listing badly to starboard, under helicopter escort, but still afloat, the *Beatrice Cenci* limped into port. She was eighteen hours late, but she was there.

The *Eleanora Duse* would be on time in New York. Unhampered by storms or cargo problems, she would be able to make up the hours she had spent standing by until certain that the *Beatrice Cenci* was able to proceed under her own steam.

It was the *Eleanora Duse*, too, who had lowered a lifeboat in search of the passenger reported overboard from her sister ship. Well known to be a largely useless gesture in such cases, it nevertheless had to be made, and the *Beatrice Cenci* was in no position to make it. The passenger, according to his documents, was one Richard Slade, a retired manufacturer, on his first visit to Europe. No effort was spared—it was most sad that the unfortunate man's holiday should have such an ending.

Until a young nurse brought certain of the *Beatrice Cenci*'s officers to have a talk with her patient, one Mrs. Abercrombie, who told a most disconcerting story. Until closer examination of the documents of the missing passenger was made and many slight discrepancies began to mount up into a most suspicious body of evidence that he could not have been what he purported. Until a most curious notation was discovered on a piece of paper hidden in the lining of his suitcase.

There was a lengthy telephone conversation between the two captains and the *Eleanora Duse* recalled her lifeboat which, in any case, was ready to return, it being far beyond the point where there could be any hope left.

Later, the captain of the *Eleanora Duse* would have a talk with the suitable American authorities. Still later, on his return voyage, the captain of the *Beatrice Cenci* would also have a lengthy talk with them, turning over the passenger's effects. The mills of justice would begin to grind, catching up a number of people who had thought themselves safe in the wealth and respectability which had been bought at the price of another's life.

"Yes," Susan said. "Perhaps I *will* visit Venice before going on to England."

"I'm glad," Ben said. And that was the consideration which deserved a bit more contemplation. He did not know of the newly-signed Will reposing in her make-up case. She had thought of it all through the long night watches while the *Beatrice Cenci* slowly ploughed her way through the deep dark ocean towards home port.

Her conclusion had been slowly arrived at, but definite. If she thought enough of Ben on such short acquaintance to draw up her Will in his favour, then perhaps she ought to give herself time to learn more about him, to get to know him better, and then decide—

She had not finished that thought. But she had decided to break her journey at Venice—Ben's first stop. After all, they might not like each other at all ashore. They might grate on each other's nerves, might discover opposing tastes about everything, might loathe each other by the end of the fortnight. Time would tell.

In the meantime, Venice lay ahead of them. That was enough to be getting on with.

"That's fine, thanks." At the foot of the gangplank, Gloria turned and repossessed Guido.

"You're sure you're all right now?" The cleric relinquished him almost reluctantly although, squirming as he was with excitement, it could not have been easy to carry him.

"Just fine. There are my relatives—just over there." She looked beyond the familiar faces, caught by the sight of several policemen converging on what looked like a perfectly innocent American tourist behind them. Drama everywhere. She wondered what he had been up to. Smuggling, perhaps, with an accomplice on board he had come to meet.

"Well, then—" The Reverend Service took a better grasp on his suitcase. "Have a nice holiday."

"Thanks. You, too." Gloria smiled at him a trifle abstractedly as she tried to quieten Guido who had got into the spirit of the occasion and was waving at everyone in sight.

Funny, her getting so uptight about the poor guy not saying Mass, when all the time he had been a Protestant clergyman. Once he'd found out what she'd been thinking, he'd come to explain to her and apologize for letting her make the mistake. Having a lot of what he called "High Church" parishioners himself, it hadn't bothered him when she kept calling him Father. And all the time she'd been suspecting— What had she been suspecting? It seemed so long ago that she hardly remembered now, the memories of shipboard life already fading.

Except for one. Poor Mr. Slade, falling overboard like that. She was going to have to make her own contacts among toy manufacturers, starting from scratch.

"Da-da!" Guido whooped, lurching away from her. "Da-da!"

"No, honey—" She pulled back on his reins. "I keep telling you—"

The answering hail brought her head up sharply. Lorenzo!

He stood there amidst the relatives, beaming. "Surprise!" they shouted in both languages.

Surprise! Gloria caught up Guido and began running towards them. *That* was what Lorenzo had been so mysteriously planning. He hadn't been firing the staff, ordering unsellable stock, bankrupting the business in her absence. He had been plotting to fly over here and surprise her.

Halted by the barrier, she signalled wildly that she

would meet them beyond Customs. They nodded agreement, throwing kisses.

"Da-da," Guido said. Not only getting it right, pointing at Lorenzo, but saying it loud enough for the relatives to hear while Lorenzo practically took bows over his brilliant son. That was the way it would be for the rest of the holiday, she supposed. Oh, well, let him take the bows, let the relatives laugh "We told you so" and tease her about the fine husband they had had to find for her. She didn't mind at all. It was going to be the best holiday she'd had in years. Surprise!

After everyone had disembarked, Val and Mrs. Abercrombie left the ship. Escorted by Angelo and another senior officer, they walked slowly to the gangplank, accommodating their strides to Mrs. Abercrombie's careful pace.

The senior officer still had the look of blank incredulity he had worn since he met Angelo carrying Mrs. Abercrombie back to her suite and had walked beside them, listening to her disjointed sentences, finally believing them.

After that, there had been the flurry of activity as numerous officers converged on the suite, listened to Mrs. Abercrombie, and disappeared again white-faced to communicate with officials ashore.

Val smiled, remembering the cold fury with which Mrs. Abercrombie had thrust the red roses into her hands and ordered her to throw them overboard. She had done so with enthusiasm and wondered if Mildred and Augustus would get the punishment they deserved. Knowing Mrs. Abercrombie, they undoubtedly would—even if it wasn't necessarily meted out by the law.

"Aaaah," Angelo sighed, mistaking the smile for something meant for him. "Bad luck. It was all very bad." His meaningful look spoke of vistas of delight snatched from them when all the alarm bells had begun to ring abruptly recalling every member of the ship's crew to duty.

This time her smile was meant for him. Let him think what he liked about where the evening might have led. It didn't matter.

What mattered was that Mrs. Abercrombie had come through it all without a relapse—in fact, it had seemed to act as a tonic to her. Furthermore, she was doing very well without the wheelchair. Which was fortunate, as the wheelchair had been so badly battered rolling about the deck that it needed vital repairs before it could be used again. Mrs. Abercrombie had donated it to the ship's sick baby. She had not intended to use it ashore anyway.

"Very bad," Angelo sighed again. "A bad voyage all the way. I wonder perhaps if this has not become a bad luck ship?"

"No," Mrs. Abercrombie paused at the head of the gangplank and looked down the deck of the *Beatrice Cenci* almost fondly. "No, I think she's a very lucky ship. We made it, didn't we?"

ABOUT THE AUTHOR

MARIAN BABSON is the author of more than twenty-five mysteries. Winner of the Poisoned Chalice and Sleuth awards, she was also a nominee for the British Gold and Silver Dagger awards. She is listed in *Publishers Weekly* as one of today's best British mystery writers. She lives in London.